DEDICATIONS

I0518708

This book is dedicated, first and foremost, to the memory of my beloved grandmother Gertrude "Trudie" Nigro, who loved the holidays, particularly Christmas, and was also a fan of the horror genre. I hope to proudly carry on the legacy she left the family as best I can.

This book is further dedicated to the memory of my late maternal great-grandparents, Sebastian and Stella Anastasia, and their daughter, my beloved Aunt Connie, who always made the holidays special, along with the rest of the year.

Very special thanks to my colleagues, friends, and editorial team Dustin Dreyling, Kevin Heim, and Matt Hickman for going above and beyond a second year in a row to ensure this tome was completed on a very tight schedule. Their hard work made the completion of this book a tremendously appreciated Christmas gift not only to this author, but also to every reader who may enjoy it (and I hope you are many!).

Table of Contents

YULETIDE HORRORS

Volume 2

Christofer Nigro

with Dustin Dreyling

Cover design & formatting:
Elden Ardiente of Lungga Creatives

©2022 Wild Hunt Press. All rights reserved. No part of this publication may be reproduced, distributed, or transmitted in any form or by any means, including photocopying, recording, or other electronic or mechanical methods, without the prior written permission of the publisher, except in the case of brief quotations embodied in critical reviews and certain other noncommercial uses permitted by copyright law. For permission requests, write to the publisher, who can be reached at the following email address: wildhuntpress@gmail.com. All events depicted in this work are fictional, and any resemblance to real individuals and events are coincidental or with non-malicious satirical intent. All pictures used are copyright their respective holders and are reproduced here for demonstrative purposes only and within legal bounds of fair use. All stories and artwork within are copyright the respective authors and artists. All original characters depicted are copyright their respective owners.

PREFACE

You may not know my name, and that is quite acceptable, for I never had much use for one of those. Unlike members of your mortal race, instead of names I've had avatars and guises, personifying different concepts that govern the universe, manifesting wherever needed and doing what needed to be done in each instance. I am not known to speak, for my presence alone and the simple gestures I make speak a universal language to all who encounter me.

Call me whatever my avatar may personify in your mind at any given time, whether it be Death or the Reaper, in which guises I have wooed cosmic beings; sought to destroy a Vampire Lord; worked in the service of a Vampire Lord (or so he believed); influenced global culture via the expression of music through a group known as the Wyld Stallyns; merged with a grim motorcyclist to claim souls through a brutal covert demolition derby; and many more. I have struck terror in the hearts of men when I made my solemn appearances and brought mercy to the suffering. I have been part of numerous personification ensembles, from the Dreaming to the Horseman of the Apocalypse.

Today, however, you can call me the Ghost of Christmas Future, where I am part of a different, triune ensemble. As such I am connected to a powerful season of the year, one that encapsulates much of the month of December, and correlates with the chill of winter and the ascendancy of darkness over the day. If that brings you chills, I have no complaints; but more than that, consider me a teacher and a shaper and shower of things that may very well come to be. Dickens recorded a classic example of my service as part of this particular grouping, and in this volume you will be made privy to yet another.

Though I do not speak as such, for fear of making uncertain outcomes far too certain, I have been known to *write* (the forbidden library of the Mansion of the Macabre is filled with my

1

scrawlings. And for those who can read and care to do so, my words may amount to profound wisdom, diatribes to chill the soul, stern lectures of warning to those who may be running afoul... or simple introductions, which is currently the case.

That all brings me to the volume you are now holding. Allow me to give you a glimpse of its contents, that you may choose to read them and thus diverge a future where your base of knowledge includes the horrific happenings within its pages.

First is "Don't Krampus my Style," where a young man named Colin Reynolds and his Uncle Ned, residents of a remote cabin in the woods of Maine, come face to face with a legendary monster of the season that brings them anything but good tidings on one particularly dark Christmas Eve.

That will next bring you to "She Had a Tail," a story occurring in those very same woods, on that very same day, that will introduce you to another legendary horror connected to the season of cold and darkness. The being in question is a lady that is, well, *no lady*, as the saying goes. Three young boys out on a Christmas Eve hunting trip with their two favorite uncles are about to encounter a nightmare from a foreign land and time that will ruin their holiday in the most bloody fashion imaginable. This tale also includes a cat, but one that you should most certainly refrain from petting.

This in turn will be followed by "Blood Carol," where the story of Colin Reynolds continues. In this tale the Ghosts of Christmas Past, Present, and Future return to show him the bloody reality of days gone by that explains his uncle's loathing of Christmas; a present that highlights the horrific reality their lives have now become; and a hint towards subsequent days that may be their salvation or their nightmarish doom. With time being of the essence, such as it always is for mortals, no opportunity will be afforded for the gentle introductions of a herald the likes of Jacob Marley; Mr. Reynolds.

The quadrilogy of terror is rounded out by "Christmas Combat," as the horrors featured in the previous three stories converge against both the survivors of these tales and upon each other for the holiday battle of the century, with the end coming from a most startling and appropriate new player.

Additionally, you may gaze upon two standalone tales included as a bonus to show that Spirits like myself, however incomprehensible to mortal minds, are not without the equivalent of generosity. "Nero: A Haunted Holiday" brings you a most unusual Christmas Eve exploit of the young werewolf Mike Nero, the star (if you can call him that) of Wild Hunt Press's *Nero* series of novels chronicling his tragic saga beginning with his younger years in the early 1980s.

The latter five yarns were all brought to you through the pen of Christofer Nigro, but the new bonus story is courtesy of author Dustin Dreyling. "Cumulus25 and the Crank: A Santa Claus Tale" brings you a most offbeat and uniquely unsettling bit of flash fiction featuring the jolly old guy in a not so jolly incarnation alongside what may be called a very strange device.

That is all you need to know and all I shall reveal at this point. Your future beckons, its nature determined by whether or not you choose to turn the pages and continue reading…

DON'T KRAMPUS MY STYLE

"I fucking hate Christmas!" Ned Reynolds decreed as he sat across from nephew and roommate Colin sipping a can of Classic Panther Pilsner beer.

"Yeah, I know, Unc," Colin said in a tone tinged with both sorrow and frustration as he threw a few small logs into the fireplace of their shared cabin.

"What the fuck ya doin' now?"

"I'm setting up a yule fire because, well, it's Yule tomorrow. Not all of us hate it."

"Kid, you need to stop worryin' about shit like that and…"

"Become a cynical prick who believes in drinking himself into a stupor as usual, instead of celebrating what Christmas stands for?"

"You know it. Life sucks, and I'm gonna celebrate its suckishness. Can you bring me another brew?"

"Get it yourself, Unc. I'm trying to light a fire for us here."

"The best way to light my fire is to get me another brew. This can here is empty." Ned belched loudly as he crumpled the tin can in his hands. A thin trickle of what was left of the beer dribbled out and onto the rug.

"Shit. There was a 'lil bit left in there."

"And now it's on the rug!" Colin griped as he went to the kitchen to get a wet paper towel.

"Get me another brew while you're in there, would ya?"

"Unc…"

Both were interrupted by a loud banging on the thick oaken front door.

"Who th' holy fucking hell could that be?" Ned queried aloud. "We live in the middle of fucking nowhere."

"I doubt it's Santa Claus paying us a visit," Colin whispered to himself in response as he soaked a paper towel in hot water from

4

the kitchen sink. "I don't see him paying *this* place a visit. More's the shame."

However, answering the door did elicit a smile on Ned Reynolds's scruffy face. Colin hated when his uncle smiled for a variety of reasons, the two main ones being: it showed off his three unsightly rotten front teeth; and it meant that he was up to no good.

"Boys!" the middle-aged hater of Christmas exclaimed as he saw his two best – and pretty much only – friends in the world, Dack and Berry, standing in the doorway.

"Merry Christmas, Mother Fucker!" they both said in tandem as they trudged in, warmly embraced Ned with their cold hands, and trudged snow onto the rug.

"Damn," Colin said quietly as he walked into the front room of the cabin. *"Them."* He then raised his voice. "Guys, please take off your boots before…"

They didn't and managed to leave wet footprints over much of the carpet as they trekked into the front room with each holding a six-pack of beer.

"We're here to celebrate the holidays with your favorite brew!" Dack exclaimed. "Twelve cans of Jekyll Island!"

"Say what?" Ned mumbled while crinkling his gray eyes in displeasure. "My brew of choice is Panther Pilsner. Panther all the way, mother fuckers! All the times we got shit-faced together, and you didn't remember that?"

"Hell no, we didn't," Berry interjected, "'cause we two are in the habit of drinking whatever brew is cheapest and on hand. And you're gonna do the same!"

"I guess I will," Ned remarked in resignation, happy to have any brew of beer offered free of charge, along with the company of some fellow alcoholics to celebrate any old thing with. "Maybe this Christmas is gonna be good after all. Ha! Ha!"

"Wonderful," Colin whispered aloud.

The young man didn't care for his uncle, let alone what passed for his friends, and the feeling was mutual. But both were the only family the other had, and the two needed to share expenses, so they tolerated each other's presence within this lonely cabin in the woods. Colin loved Christmas and what it stood for, yearning for the magickal, hopeful days of celebration he enjoyed in his childhood when he had more family and a more stable life. This particular thing, however, was most definitely *not* mutual between him and Uncle Ned.

"I see your nephew was nice enough to light a fire for us," Berry said as he sat his fat ass down in one of the front room chairs. "He must have known we were comin'! Really thoughtful of the kid!"

"Yeah, right!" Dack said as he and the other three laughed in tandem. "It was a happy fucking accident, but shit, I'll take it!" The three men laughed in between gulps of two brands of beer between them.

"This shit is good, but I really wish we had some Schraderbrau," Berry noted, "imported dee-rectly from New Mexico. Along with some of the blue rocks I heard you can get there. All the best shit comes from New Mexico!"

"Well, this is Maine, not New Mexico, and we're out in the middle of the boonies," Ned stated as he took another swig of his Panther. "So, you get what you can get here, right?"

"Yup," Dack and Berry said simultaneously as they both drank to that.

Then again, they would drink to just about anything.

Colin finally stepped into the sad spectacle he saw before him. "You know, instead of drinking… this, I wish I could just get you gents some eggnog or cocoa. That's much more in the spirit of Christmas."

"Nah, that shit has too much sugar," Berry griped. "What are you tryin' to do, kill us or somethin'? Hah! Hah!"

"Your nephew is funny," Dack said as he chugged down the remainder of his first can of beer before setting the empty container on the nearby end table and reaching for another.

"You think he's so fucking funny, then maybe I'll send him to live with *you,*" Ned commented.

"Fuck, no!" Dack retorted. "I like to actually enjoy myself, 'specially on fucking Christmas!"

The three friends laughed again… but Colin didn't. He just pouted and began thinking very negative thoughts. About those three, their cynicism, the idea of giving up and giving in due to hard times, and a refusal to appreciate what Christmas represented and the magick its spirit could bring into their lives if they were willing to continue seeing it the way they did in their much younger years.

The young man gritted his teeth and clenched his fists, wanting to lash out at these men. Not being a violent person, however, he relented. Little did he know, however, that the forces inherent in the season were about to lash out for him.

***

No sooner did Colin think those thoughts and harbor those ill wishes, no matter how briefly, than the late afternoon sky above the lonely wilderness cabin grew darkly overcast. The snow began falling harshly, and within several minutes, it appeared as if not only was the truck shared by him and his uncle buried up to its doors, but so was the Ford Canyonero that Dack and Berry drove up in.

"Shit, you see that sudden blight of bad weather?" Berry noted while watching the window quickly become covered in white.

"Yeah, man," Ned answered. "Looks like me and the kid just got snowed in. And it looks like you fellas are stuck here with us for the Christmas weekend."

"Well, then, it's a good thing that we have enough beer between the three of us!" Dack chuckled as Berry and Ned laughed with him in agreement.

"Wonderful," Colin muttered to himself again. "Could I possibly get any worse company?"

The younger Reynolds quickly learned not to tempt fate with such rhetorical questions as all four inhabitants of the remote home were startled by a loud thump on the wooden ceiling.

"What the holy fuck?" Ned exclaimed.

"It sounded like a fucking 200-pound buck just jumped on the roof!" Berry proclaimed.

Colin was likewise spooked, and all the more so when he heard a clanking noise in the burning fireplace directly below their chimney. He turned in that direction to see what resembled a metal box with a turn crank on the side of it sitting on the burning logs.

"Did… someone just drop something down your chimney, Ned?" Dack asked with an anxious stutter.

"It looks like someone did," was the only answer Ned could give. "What the actual fuck…?"

Despite how unnerved he was, Berry was overcome with curiosity. He got up and approached the strange little metallic square that had suddenly been dumped into their midst.

"It looks like… a jack-in-the-box? I haven't had me one of those since I was just a little shit Brings back memories!"

"Watch it, man!" Dack warned. "That box has gotta be hot from fallin' in the fire!"

"Y'all don't need to mother me none," Berry replied. "I'll put a glove on to fetch it and turn the handle."

"Berry don't…" Colin pleaded, as he had a very bad feeling about the odd little gift.

"Quiet, kid," the older man responded gruffly. "You snooze, you lose. This little Christmas gift is all mine. Go pour yourself some eggnog or somethin'."

Putting on a thick glove he removed from his coat pocket, Berry pulled the tin jack-in-the-box away from the burning logs by its crank. He then began turning the lever, and grinned as it played a pleasant but oddly haunting tune. After several seconds, as expected the lid popped open and out came the titular "Jack."

This one wasn't exactly typical, however. It did have the obligatory jester with three jingling bells hat and small extended arms, but its face was not exactly joyous. Rather, it had a ghastly chalk white face that possessed leering red eyes and a gaping mouth with a forked tongue painted onto the chin.

Colin winced at the sight.

"Geez," Berry said as he looked over the grotesque little mannequin. "You're one ugly little mother fuck-"

The man's expletive was rudely cut off as a chain-like extension suddenly sprang from "Jack's" gaping mouth and entwined tightly around Berry's throat. The grip was so strong that his airway was immediately cut off and a dark purple bruise of great size appeared around the entirety of his neck.

"Holy Jesus Fuck All!" Ned screamed.

"Ned, it's choking him!" Dack cried in terror. "We've gotta do something!"

The two men jumped off their chairs and ran towards their gagging friend. Colin could only stare in startled disbelief, wanting to help but not able to fully process what he was seeing.

Before either Ned or Dack could reach Berry, the tin box did two more startling things with great quickness. One was the hands and arms of the "Jack" suddenly becoming animate and grasping the chain extending from its mouth, as if to further tighten the grip. Two was a small hatch opening in the back of the tin square, from which a second chain projected out and up the chimney.

In a third and final blur of motion, both the sinister jack-in-the-box and Berry himself were yanked off the floor and up the chimney as if the chain extending up there was pulled on by a tremendously strong force. Several pounds of gray, soot-covered snow crumpled down into the fireplace to douse the burning embers in the aftermath of a hefty grown man being pulled up the wide brick chute and evidently out onto the roof in just under a second.

"Holy shit stains!" Ned cried out at the unbelievable event.

"Berry… oh, god…" Dack murmured and fell to his knees.

Colin's mouth was open wide with horror and shock. He tried to speak while attempting to understand what was going on. As he slowly began doing so, the horror of what he may have had an inadvertent hand in unleashing on his cabin home and sole remaining family member struck him with the force of a proverbial piledriver.

Ned grabbed his weeping friend and pulled him to his feet in one mighty heave.

"Dack, you stupid fucking drunk! You've gotta get your senses back! Berry just got killed or taken or some shit, and we're gonna be next if we don't-"

They were interrupted by a crashing sound to their left. This turned out to be a tiny reddish object hurled by an unseen hand through the side window. A stream of biting cold air and sleet entered by way of the broken glass as the object suddenly "stood" up to reveal itself as a six-inch tall painted toy soldier of an identifiably classic variety. The scarlet uniform and tall furry Brigade of Guards hat was there, as was a miniature rifle with a bayonet on the end. However, the usual neutral or smiley countenance was replaced by a sulking, decidedly evil-looking sneer with a face painted ghostly white rather than skin tone pink.

The figure stiffly walked with a distinct clinking sound a few feet towards the remaining trio of men on its non-bendable legs. It then halted and pointed its toy firearm. The blade on the end suddenly parted into a triune of sharp, curved points that looked like a fishing hook-like prong. The synthetic soldier then fired the blade, which was connected to a thin metal wire on the toy rifle. The tri-bladed hook imbedded itself into Dack's lips, piercing the flesh in three separate places: two piercing the upper lip, and one clear through the middle of the bottom, all holding fast.

Dack would have screamed in agony if he could, but his mouth was hooked closed. He desperately attempted to pull the perforating object from his lips but only succeeded in escalating the amount of blood flowing out the triple puncture wound.

"Jesus!" Ned hollered. "Kid, help me get that thing out of him!"

This time Colin moved with his uncle to do just that. Before they could reach the man and do *something* to aid him, another wire extended from the top of the toy soldier's big fluffy hat and out the jagged hole that had been broken in the window. Something on the other end of that second cord then evidently yanked on the wooden mini-man, pulling both it and Dack's weighty body off the floor and out the window, smashing him through the remainder of the pane.

Ned and Colin, now startled out of their wits, could scarcely imagine the excruciating degree of pain that move must have caused the hapless Dack, considering where the prongs of the blade were affixed. They could only hope that it was as mercifully brief as it looked.

The only sound following that of their friend crashing through the glass was the shrill howling of the winter wind gushing into the house via the makeshift opening where the windowpane used to be. The floor was stained with a thick trail of blood that seeped from out of Dack's lips as he was pulled out the window., The crimson spatter was now mixing with a growing pile of snow and sleet that had blown in through the hole.

"Did... did you see that? Dack...?" was all the utterly confused and horrified Ned could get out before the next thing happened.

That next thing was the heavy front door being kicked open and off its hinges as if it weighed mere ounces. The thick-sinewed leg that did the job seemed covered in hair, and it ended not in a foot but a cloven hoof.

A towering being well over seven feet in height and clad in a tattered tan, robe-like garment and carrying a huge woolen sack on his back strode in as if he owned the place. This figure possessed massively muscular arms covered in shaggy brown hair and ending in big, clawed hands. His face was a horrid chimera of human and goat-like features with two large ram-like horns jutting from his skull. The nightmarish entity's fiery red eyes glared at the two men inside the cabin.

This demonic gaze clearly fixated on Ned, however, and the being grinned at him, showing rows of sharpened teeth. A long, serpent-like tongue extended from his maw and wriggled as if tasting the air inside the cabin. The being's fetid breath could be detected from several feet away.

"It's... it's the fucking Devil..." Ned stammered.

"No, not exactly..." Colin nervously replied, accurately deducing the actual identity of the dark being they now beheld.

The young man dashed in front of his trembling uncle in a protective stance. Ned began inching back towards a desk where he kept his hunting rifle handy.

"Leave my uncle alone!" Colin screamed at the Krampus. "You already took his friends! Take *me* instead of him! It's my fault that you're here, not his!"

"Wrong…" the being uttered in a deeply coarse voice while pointing his crooked, clawed index finger in the direction of Uncle Ned. "You *all* called me. But *he* lacks… the true spirit. *Not you.*"

"No! You stay away from him!" Colin yelled.

"Kid, get out the fucking way!" he heard Ned holler from behind.

Colin jumped aside as he pointed the loaded rifle at the hulking intruder. He pulled the trigger and a .204 Ruger caliber bullet – sufficient to take down a coyote – struck the hairy beast in his right shoulder. A spurt of dark blood spilled out of the wound as the impact knocked the Krampus back into the wall near the broken door. The younger Reynolds shouted in defiance as he grabbed a metal poker from the fireplace and attacked the monstrous home invader with it.

He struck the Krampus twice with the metal object, showing an impressive degree of force for a slight, non-violent person. It failed to have the desired effect, however. The dark Anti-Santa swatted him across the room as a human might an offending fly. Ned released another shot, and it struck its target in the chest. The Krampus grumbled in pain as more blood spurted from yet another gaping wound, but annoyance was the dominant look in his eyes.

Even these two direct hits from a hunting rifle were insufficient to put a serious crimp in the Krampus, however. The beastly creature retaliated by opening his sack and dumping what looked like a bright red toy fire engine on the cabin floor. This miniature vehicle lit up and began wheeling towards Ned while emitting a motorized whine. He began haphazardly aiming the rifle, not sure which of the two targets to focus on, until the toy truck took matters out of his hands by extending what looked like a tiny hose from its front section.

This tube spewed what seemed to be a stream of corrosive liquid that hit the barrel of the rifle, both gumming up the chamber and rapidly deforming the metal so it could no longer fire. Some of the fluid got on Ned's hands and created burning blisters that caused him to shout and drop the weapon. The Krampus ran towards the older Reynolds with a speed that belied the entity's great size, then lifted him into the air as effortlessly as a person may do with a pillow and stuffed the large man completely into the sack.

"No!" Colin yelled from across the room as he recovered his senses and pulled himself to his feet. "You won't take my uncle! He's all I've got!"

"Not anymore…" the Krampus grumbled cynically as he rushed out the front door with Ned inside the sack.

"Nooooo…!"

Colin swiftly stepped into some snowshoes and grabbed his thick winter coat as he followed outside into the freezing winds. However, he saw nothing besides the blowing snow and glimpses of the waving branches of the trees. The fast-moving frozen precipitation stung his eyes and bit into his skin like millions of tiny needles. He went trudging through several feet of snow, braving the blustery conditions and straining to see more than a few feet in front of him due to the darkness of the hour and the white-out conditions.

The young man kept running for what seemed like hours and it may have been that long. But he found nothing and saw nothing save more snow careening through the harsh winds like an undulating white blanket that made his skin feel like walking ice.

END

SHE HAD A TAIL

Of all the things twelve-year-old Dillon Lumpkin could be doing in the late evening hours of Christmas Eve, his uncles Dandridge and Kenton were taking him and his two same-aged cousins, Gavin and Laurel, hunting. The cold mountain wilderness of northern Maine was a perfect place to do this, and the sparsely populated area was filled with a relatively recent influx of immigrants of ancient Teutonic descent who preferred to live much as their ancestors did. Besides, wi-fi and cell phone reception out here in the boonies really sucked, and shooting game was more fun than blasting fake pixelated targets in a video game anyway.

What Dillon didn't want to mention was his trepidation in being out there that day, based on what his younger sister Thea claimed to have seen days earlier.

The girl alleged to have looked out the window a week prior during a particularly bad overnight snowstorm to see someone strange walk past the back of the house. What she described was a "tall but really beefy older lady in old-ass clothing, like something out of the Middle Ages or some far off time like that." She seemed unbothered by the biting cold wind and trudged through the several feet of snow on the ground as if it presented no obstacle. And she did so while evidently wearing no winter clothing, and nothing but thin sandals on her feet.

"She was wrinkly and really ugly looking and had this really long-ass scraggly hair, kinda like me when I have a really bad hair day and it gets all frizzed out and shit. But really, *really* gray. That lady was gangly but big, and she walked like she was a queen or something, like she owned the whole forest. It's hard to explain, I guess, but that's what I thought while seeing her. And… and…"

Thea seemed to hesitate about the next detail.

"And what else are you trying to tell me?" Dillon asked his trembling little sibling.

14

"Well, um… she had a tail. Like the kind a lizard has."

"Seriously, Thea? C'mon now! Have you been sneaking into Mom's liquor cabinet? Or scarfing down too many of Aunt Jenny's baked good 'edibles'?"

"No! I'm serious, Dillon! She… she had a tail! I saw it sticking out of her dress, sliding behind her on the snowy ground! It was a tail!"

Dillon had no idea what to make of that last detail, let alone who this strange and obviously scary-looking old woman could have been, but he passed the sighting off as some odd new neighbor with Alzheimer's who may have wandered out into the storm and gotten lost. The whipping winds and late hour made Thea mistake a dangling piece of clothing for a tail and may have exaggerated other features of this strange, unfamiliar person.

But he still remembered how his little sis trembled and how teary-eyed she got when she described who – what – she had seen. He never noticed such an old lady wandering around the vicinity of their home before or since, but some of his immigrant neighbors in the thinly populated region were newcomers to the wilderness area. Could it be that people of old world Icelandic descent dress differently, and have fewer problems with the cold even on a night when blizzard conditions are brewing?

The boy tried to put such thoughts out of his head and enjoy the impromptu hunting trip he was on, courtesy of a Christmas weekend visit from his two crazy and outdoorsy uncles.

"Thanks for this neat ass Christmas gift!" Gavin said as he plowed his feet through the thick snow beside his two cousins. "It was lots better than the early presents Dillon and I got!"

"Let me guess," Uncle Dandridge replied. "You two were given clothes! Ha! Ha! I always hated that shit when I was a kid!"

"We sure as hell did!" Gavin confirmed. "Me, Dillon, and Thea! New 'stylish' shit we're expected to wear to school when the holiday vacation is over! Only Laurel was lucky enough not to get new clothes of any kind! He got an Xbox! Lucky little prick. Everyone in the family 'cept for you two like him more than Dillon and me."

15

"Oh, stop being such a dick!" Laurel exclaimed. "They know I like video games, and you and Dillon never played any. And I'm hard to fit with clothes anyways, so they didn't know what to get me."

"Bullshit," Gavin retorted. "You'd be bitching too if all you got was new clothes."

"Okay, enough, you guys!" Dillon stepped in. "This is Christmas Eve, we don't need to be squabbling. The Uncs are taking us on a hunting trip, so let's shoot some rabbits for dinner with the family tonight. You know how much my Mom hates cooking, 'specially for so many people. And... well, I really think we should stick together. There can be... dangerous people out here."

"Kid, the only dangerous people out here in these woods are us," Uncle Kenton said while wiping snowflakes off his bushy beard. "We're five men carrying fucking rifles, so we're deadlier than a whole pack of wolves. What could be out here that we should be worried about? You thinking maybe some evil old rabbit will jump us? Ha! Ha!"

"No," Dillon responded. "You just never know who some of our new neighbors might be, that's all."

"You mean some of the Germies?" Gavin asked. "They don't come around much. Some of them are old as fuck, anyway, and probably couldn't even lift a rifle to save their lives. But maybe we *should* be careful, 'cause they might still be able to throw snowballs at us."

Uncles Dandridge and Kenton started laughing uproariously alongside Gavin. Laurel remained quiet and simply shook his head. He was always the "good" boy of the related bunch. Gavin was the troublemaker, and Dillon took pride as the tough but studious one. Being such a scholar-aborning, after what Thea mentioned to him, he began doing some research about Teutonic folklore and culture on the Internet, when the intermittent wi-fi out here allowed it. He had the following question that he wanted answered:

If this recent slew of immigrants still hold to their old world customs and legends,"

16

, what else from their native land may have come along with them?

What he learned was this: Images from Icelandic folklore of strange old women with tails pointed to a terrifying being. However, he kept telling himself that Thea's description of that detail was just a weird coincidence based on a mistake she must have made due to unfavorable sighting conditions.

Dillon then screamed in horror as something hit him hard on his right arm. He turned and pointed his rifle defensively in that direction.

It turned out that it was just Gavin having hurled a snowball at him. "Easy, easy, bro! I was just shittin' around!"

"Dillon!" Uncle Kenton hollered. "Don't you ever point that fucking rifle at one of us! What's the matter with you, guy?"

Laurel was staring with a dumbfounded expression. "Dillon... lower that gun. Y'know, maybe we should call this whole thing off. I didn't think Dillon could get spooked like that."

"I'm sorry," Dillon lamented. "I just got nervous, that's all."

"Well, you need to stop being so nervous and start being more aware of your surroundings," Uncle Dandridge noted. "Hunting can be dangerous, and we can be dangerous to each other if we aren't responsible. These rifles are not toys, man!"

"I know, I know," Dillon said. "I'm sorry, okay? I said I was sorry. It's just... well, last week Thea saw... someone strange out here. And I did some research, and, well..."

"Oh no, not more of that fucking studying of yours," Gavin remarked with rolling eyes. "Maybe you actually *should* just shoot me now."

"Gavin, shut up!" Laurel shouted.

That was when the group heard a sudden rustling in the thickets located just a few feet away. The most enormous cat that any of them had ever seen exploded out of the foliage and disappeared behind a huge snowbank at blurring speed. The animal moved fast, but the group saw just enough of it to realize it was not something that should be in those woods... or even in this world.

17

"Shit! Did you see that?" Gavin spouted while pointing his rifle at the now vanished aberration. "Did… did we just see a panther?"

"There are no panthers in these woods!" Uncle Dandridge said, unable to conceal the fact that he, too, was unnerved by what they had just witnessed.

"And aren't panthers black?" Laurel asked. "I saw that thing, and… it was more like a grayish, smokey color. Maybe it was a puma or something?"

"Pumas are very rare, and likely not even around this part of the country," Dillon explained. "And their coats are tan, not black or gray, or… dark at all."

"But it looked like a cat!" Gavin insisted. "A really big ass, ugly ass cat! Maybe it was a lynx?"

"A lynx doesn't get that big," Uncle Kenton mentioned as he checked his rifle to make sure it was properly loaded. "And they have just a little knob for a tail. That… cat we saw had a really long tail."

"But it was really a cat of some kind, then?" Laurel queried nervously.

"You saw the damn thing too, didn't you?" Gavin replied anxiously.

"I did," Laurel retorted, "but… well, it moved really fast, and…"

"It *was* some kind of cat," Dillon confirmed as he readied his rifle. "I saw it. I know what I saw. But bigger than any cat should have been."

"Dillon is right," Uncle Dandridge noted. "I saw what he saw. We all did. But let's not worry. There are five of us here, and we're all armed. But maybe we should head back to the cabin now."

"Do we have to, Uncle Dandridge?" Gavin griped. "Maybe we can find that thing and shoot it. Imagine what we could get for a carcass like that?"

"I think Unc is right, Gav," Dillon interjected. "I've got a bad feeling about things."

Just then the group heard another sound behind a big spruce tree located just up a snow-covered hill. They turned to see a very tall, rather hideous looking old crone peeking out from behind it. She was holding up a small furry object with a large but thin bony hand. It soon become clear that it was a headless hare with several human-looking bites taken out of it. Blood dribbled down from the stump where part of its severed vertebrae was visible, indicating that the kill was a fresh one.

"You gentleman are hunting rabbits for dinner, yes?" the horrible hag asked in a hoarse voice with a slight Icelandic accent. "I caught one for you. I already ate some of it, however. I hope you do not mind. Hee. Hee. Hee…"

"What the fuck!" Gavin screamed.

The horrific sight made it instantly clear that this "old woman" couldn't possibly be human. Accordingly, in a state of panic the boy pointed his rifle at the haggish being and fired.

The bullet struck the hare's corpse, causing it to splatter in what resembled a small explosion of scarlet. The crone-like lady holding it darted behind the tree with a speed that seemed completely unnatural for a withered old woman to display. She cackled loudly while doing so, as if the whole tableau was amusing to her.

As she disappeared behind the tree, Dillon could swear he saw a long, ropey tail slithering in back of her.

"Oh… my god," he said quietly to himself. "It's… Gryla."

"Who the what?" Uncle Dandridge said as he likewise checked his rifle. "Who the fuck was that old bitch? How could she move like that? Did she… did she kill and eat that rabbit raw? With its skin still on it?"

"Gryla," Dillon responded, "is some type of powerful witch or female ogre, from Teutonic mythology. She's connected to the winter, and to the season of Christmas. She… must have followed the belief patterns, or whatever, of the Icelandic immigrants who came here. And… that means the animal we saw must have been the Yule Cat. God help us, please…"

"What do you mean, Dillon?" Laurel inquired while trembling for reasons that had nothing to do with the cold weather. "Only a few of those immigrants settled a few miles from here! The only other cabin near here is the one where Ned Reynolds and his nephew live"

"Don't you feel it in the cold winter air?" Dillon asked as he prepared his rifle for defense. "There's all this… dark seasonal energy building up in this region for some reason. I read about how that can happen. All sorts of things can manifest here now. We're in a world of shit. And so is everyone else around these woods."

"Dillon, cut it out, okay?" Laurel pleaded.

"No, I think the kid might be onto something," Uncle Kenton said, "because I can swear I've felt… something weird in the air too. We need to get back to the cabin now. Keep your wits about you, 'cause it's about a half mile back."

"You are not going to make it," came Gryla's deep, scratchy voice from behind them.

The group turned to see the towering haggish entity standing boldly in all her grotesquely aged glory just a few feet from them. She looked much as both little Thea Lumpkin and the chronicles of Icelandic folklore had described her: well-built but very elderly looking, with classic "old crone" features including an ugly, wrinkled, war-covered face adorned with a long pointy nose sporting a bulbous excrescence on the tip. Her long, unkempt hair was grayish-white, and she had an old-style kerchief tied around her forehead. The rest of her attire looked weathered and well-worn, to say the least, and resembled a medieval chemise gown. Her feet wore nothing to protect them from the sub-zero snow piled on the ground besides a pair of worn-out looking sandals.

Standing beside the seven-foot-crone was an animal of feline pedigree but roughly the size of a bull, very likely the one which the group had seen at the beginning of the nightmare now unfolding before them. The Yule Cat resembled less a panther than a wild beast with a basic cat-like design, sporting nearly iridescent yellow eyes and a mouthful of razor-like teeth that would make a lion envious. These were easily discernible as the animal raised her back and hissed viciously with her mouth gaping wide, eager to pounce on some prey at any moment.

20

"Holy shit on a stick," Uncles Dandridge and Kenton said simultaneously.

The sinister supernatural feline's gaze was obviously fixed upon Laurel. And for a good reason.

Gryla suddenly sported a noxious grin. "Did I hear you say that *this boy* was the only one amongst yon kids to *not* receive a new set of clothing for Christmas? My pet here can sense that quite clearly." The whole party cringed, as they realized it had gotten so late that the time must have slipped just past midnight into Christmas day.

Knowing this, Gryla followed the Yule Cat's gaze to Laurel, and she patted the animal on her shaggy grayish neck. "He is all yours, my precious pet."

Before any of the group could react, the Yule Cat leapt over ten feet at them, landing on Laurel and slamming him onto the snowy ground. The cacophony of the boy's screams were almost drowned out by the sounds of the feline tearing his thick winter clothing and flesh to shreds with a combination of her claws and teeth as the animal ravenously fed.

Uncles Dandridge and Kenton recovered from their shock and pointed their rifles. The former released a shot that struck the Yule Cat just over her right front leg. The animal snarled in pain, jumped off her prey, and dashed into a clump of shrubbery. The latter fired another shot into the snow-covered greenery but could not be certain if he hit their target a second time.

It was too late, however. Laurel was now clearly a corpse, his eyes frozen open and mouth gaping wide with his throat torn out and stomach opened up with glistening internal organs exposed. The snow gleamed a wet red all around his mutilated form.

"Oh my god!" Gavin shouted. "Laurel!"

Dillon's mouth dropped low, struggling to accept the reality of what he knew was going on around him, and what the remainder of his family was now facing.

Unfortunately for his uncles, both had to turn their backs on Gryla to shoot at the Yule Cat. This gave the mighty winter witch more than enough time to move on them with a sudden bolt of

21

motion. Standing inches taller than both men, she first grabbed Kenton by his neck and lifted him in the air as if he weighed mere ounces. She took a bite out of his pharynx and swallowed the chunk of flesh right away.

"Tastes better than the rabbit did," she said, her thin lips and sharpened teeth caked with the man's blood. "But could still use a bit of seasoning."

Uncle Dandridge bellowed in terror and pointed his rife at the horrendous hag. But it was for naught, as Gryla's strength and reflexes far outmatched his own. In a single spin of motion, she tossed the dead body of Kenton aside and swatted Dandridge's piece from his hands.

The ogress grasped each side of his face in her hands and tore his head clean off. She then lifted his body effortlessly above her head, flipped the carcass upside down, and opened her mouth wide to catch the fountain of blood pouring out of the stump like a can of spilled scarlet milk. She shook the body as she did so to ensure that she get every last possible drop.

"Waste not, want not," the winter witch said after looking at the mortified Dillon and Gavin with a pernicious grin as she licked the dripping crimson of Uncle Dandridge's life fluid off her mouth. "A *final* lesson for you and yours, lads. All thanks to your dear Auntie Gryla. Hee. Hee. Hee."

"Let's get that bitch!" Gavin screamed as he pointed his hunting rifle after the legendary ogress of the snow.

Dillon followed suit without hesitation.

Gryla found herself assaulted by a salvo of high caliber lead. She grumbled in pain and rage as a series of bloody entry wounds appeared on her arms and gut, along with a particularly nasty perforation on the side of her shriveled neck. Dark blood seeped out of each bullet hole in her flesh as she sprinted off behind a large snowbank at such speed that the last few shots failed to hit her.

"She killed our uncles!" Gavin shouted with naked rage. "Her fucking cat killed Laurel!"

"Gavin!" Dillon yelled while grabbing his sibling's arm and shaking him to his senses. "Get hold of yourself and reload your fucking gun! Hurry!"

As both of the youths did so, all they heard in response was Gryla's guttural voice echoing from somewhere beyond the trees where she now stood hidden.

"You boys are very bad. You would try to deny your Auntie Gryla the food that she and her precious little pet are due every winter. That is no way to treat your elders, those of us who were old when your kind first appeared on this world. You are, as your kind might say, below us on the food chain, and you will show us that due respect. So, your auntie is going to teach you *another* much-needed lesson, and truly the last you will ever receive.

"I am not going to grant you the fast death I gave to the others in your company. Instead, I am going to give you a head start, and I will hunt you down like the wretched little scamps you are as you attempt to get back to your little wooden home. Needless to say, you shan't reach it... intact. Hee. Hee. Hee."

"You stupid old bitch!" Gavin hollered as he pointed the rifle in the general direction that Gryla's voice was emanating from. "Come out where we can see you and face us like... well, like the tough old bitch you think you are!"

Dillon stifled the move by pushing the gun barrel down. "Gavin, save your ammo 'till we can see her or that fucking cat-thing of hers! Wasting ammo is exactly what she wants us to do!"

Gavin ceased as requested, trembling in the wake of the horrific events that had just claimed the life of three family members right in front of him. He also had the stark realization that the same fate now awaited him and Gavin as well... albeit slower and with even less mercy.

"Dillon... we're not gonna make it, are we?"

"Maybe not. But for the sake of Laurel and our uncles... we've gotta try."

Gavin nodded in agreement despite the look of complete terror and shock on his face. The two lads then lifted their rifles at the ready as they began trekking through the deep snow and chilling

23

winds over the half mile distance leading towards Dillon's cabin home.

The boys were quite aware that it may as well have been a thousand miles away.

END

BLOODY CAROL

Colin Reynolds trudged through several feet of snow in the middle of the dark wilderness of Maine this Christmas Eve. He barely had time to step into winter boots and hastily grab the first winter coat on the rack when he fled his cabin into the blizzard conditions of this winter night. The young man was seeking out his Uncle Ned, who had been ripped out of his life, and quite literally from the remote home they shared, by a dark being – perhaps more a force of nature, a walking shadowy archetype of the season – that he previously believed to exist only in legend.

He believed this, as most people do, because until Christmas Eve of this year, he had lived a normal life and entertained a worldview that did not accommodate certain things. Specifically, the things that we take for granted as only existing in our nightmares, of populating the pages of books and the screens of cinema & television that are designed to scare us with horrific images that cannot threaten us for real.

While many of us are told that God and angels exist, other nebulous beings are not supposed to. Entities like the Catholic saints, including St. Nicholas, are said to be real... but Santa Claus isn't. And despite his being one of St. Nick's guises?

Of course, as Colin mused, we're also told that the Devil is supposed to be real. So... if he is real, and St. Nick is real, then why not Santa Claus? And, for that matter... why not the Krampus? Especially since it was the latter being that snatched Uncle Ned away, after first doing the same to two friends of his while downing brewskis in celebration of a holiday they didn't actually respect.

Colin did honor the season, however, despite the lack of belief in what it represented by his uncle. He and Ned may not have cared for each other as people, or saw eye to eye on most anything, but they were all the other had left of family (save for one now

25

residing in a hospital for the mentally ill, but surely she didn't count). He thought it was his own negative feelings projected at his uncle and his two friends' drunken behavior that caused the Krampus to come down on them. In actuality, however, it was revealed that their cynicism of the season was more than enough to do so during a time and place when these potent energies were, for unknown reasons, particularly concentrated this season.

Now evidently being left alone in the world, and in such a horrific manner that he felt partly responsible for it, Colin was compelled to find and rescue his uncle. After all, isn't that something any decent person would do anyway, especially on the late evening hours heading into Christmas day?

But he had no idea where the Krampus took the people he snatched and even less how to find it. He looked in every direction of the blizzard-ridden forest around him, calling Ned's name over and over in futile fashion. Now beginning to freeze, his nearly insanity-driven will was no longer sufficient to brave these blustery conditions that no human was suited to withstand.

Praying was the only other thing he could think of doing besides collapsing in the snow and allowing the weather to claim him. He was no longer a devout Christian, but he both silently and verbally pleaded to St. Nicholas, the spirit of Christmas, to please *please* help him. To do *something* for him.

But as he fell to the frost-covered ground, he knew that only Death would be coming for him, and his uncle would be trapped in the clutches of the Krampus forever… whether that be in Hell, or some nether-realm that the dark Christmas entity had carved out for himself.

Suddenly, the feeling of the biting wind and sub-zero temperatures ceased. A brief sense of calm overtook Colin. The rifle he took from the cabin was still in his grasp, as he could clearly feel its metal barrel under his fingers. Several seconds later, he had the courage to open his eyes. At first, he seemed to be in a blank, darkened chamber that was lit by a rapidly growing illumination. That light grew more intense until its source was revealed as a strange being materializing before him.

26

This entity was rather diminutive in size, with an aura that suggested both young and unspeakably ancient. Whether it was male or female was actually difficult to say, but it had an almost cherubic face with long locks of silvery hair, adding to the dichotomy of age surrounding it. The Spirit being's arms and legs were surprisingly brawny, and they were readily visible since the entity was garbed in a white tunic festooned with a tight, shimmery belt. In its right hand was a small branch with green leaves on the end, which some could identify as a sprig of holly.

"Greetings, Colin Reynolds," the Spirit said in a gentle voice. "You need fear nothing… for the moment. I have transported you out of the conditions that would have soon spelled doom for one of your race."

"Who… who the hell are you?" Colin asked as he gripped his rifle tightly.

"You will not need the weapon, and it will do you no good if you did attempt bringing it to bear upon me," the glowing Spirit replied. "I allowed you to retain it simply for whatever security it may provide you, and because you shall likely need it later, in a different place."

"Who. The. Fuck. Are. You?"

"Tut, tut with the needless hostility. You may simply call me the Ghost of Christmas Past. I came to you because you called out to the forces that govern me… and many others of note. The conditions of your material environment have many seasonal forces converging on it, and one fortunate result was your pleas for succor being able to effectively reach Us."

"Us?"

"Yes… me and two others of Spirit who are in some ways bound to each other in a triune chain of magick, of the sort that binds other such separate beings together. The Holy Trinity, the Triple Goddess, the Norns… I could go on, but I believe I have made my point to one of your doubtless limited understanding."

"So… you came to rescue me? To help me find my uncle?"

"In a manner of speaking. But it shan't be so easy, I am afraid. The aid of We Three comes with a price, one that is paid in lessons to be learned and experiences to be endured."

"Of course, it would be." Colin sighed. "Who are those other two? Wait... you can't mean those guys from *A Christmas Carol*? They aren't real!"

"To the contrary, the mortal author Charles Dickens took the account of our meeting directly from Ebenezer Scrooge. He felt obliged to let the reading public believe it was a work of fiction, so he was not accused of spreading a silly falsehood."

"I... guess I can believe that, considering how the Krampus turned out to be real. So, what do I have to do, or experience, or whatever, in order to get help in getting my uncle the fuck away from the Krampus?"

"You shall meet my fellow two in due course, as we manifest one at a time, each following the other in linear order according to the calendar of time your race is accustomed. As for what you must experience as part of receiving the important aid that we offer... well, I am pleased that you asked that. The process leading to it will now begin to unfold."

***

Colin Reynolds perceived a brief moment of darkness, and next he was standing on his two feet, rifle in hand, beholding a city street that was instantly recognizable to him. It was the small metropolis of London, Maine, located in Penobscot County just south of the town of Derry. The two-apartment home that he grew up in, with his Uncle Ned living in the unit downstairs, stood directly in front of Colin and the Spirit.

However, he quickly noticed details suggesting that this was his home from a time many years in the past. Everything was covered in snow, and the decorations outside were clearly indicative of how his mother would embellish the place during the Christmas season.

Colin looked to the end of the block to see a relic from long ago days: the small corner store with the half-faded blue sign that read 'Fittinger's Tasty Treats.'

"But it can't be!" he declared.

"But it is," the Spirit responded. "You know where you are, but you are not there as it is in what you consider the present. This is the past, which is my purview. The time is a Christmas that you once knew, as both you and your Uncle Ned used to experience it."

"Seriously, man? But there are a few people walking by... people I used to know! I recognize Randy Simmons right there, including that hand-me-down Black Bears coat he liked so much. But why don't they react to us, with me holding this gun, and you... well, looking the way you do?"

"We are outside the linear progression of things, as you recall them. You can witness events as they happened but cannot act upon what you see. Similarly, none from that era, including your counterpart native to it, can see either of us."

"This... this is fucking insane! But... why...?"

"Because you must see this to understand your uncle better. Specifically, why he became so distasteful of the Christmas images you revere and the meaning of the day, and thus became prone to harm by the darker forces connected to this season when present under conditions that favored their manifestation. You will bear witness to some of what you remember, and other events you were never aware of."

The Spirit gestured for Colin to follow and the two walked literally through the front door of the house without opening it. Inside was what the latter recalled as a festive event, mostly full of people that were no longer with him. His expression was aghast as he saw his seven-year-old self sitting in one of the chairs of the big dining room table. It was full of tasty foods and a few 2-liter bottles of soda, including a favorite of his that is no longer made, Cherry & Cream Mocha Cola.

Sharing the table with the little boy he used to be were his grandfather, his dad, his mom, a much younger and less bitter Ned, and...

29

"Uncle Monty," Colin said with a despondent tone. "Oh, man, it makes me so sad to see him again, just like I remember him. I mean, I miss him, and Ned sure as hell misses him, because he died so young. The last time I saw him alive was a Christmas gathering like this, when he and Ned had a huge argument." That was when it struck him. "Wait, is this? Oh, no…"

The Spirit gave a sympathetic nod of confirmation as Colin steeled himself for what he was about to witness. Or, rather, *re-witness.*

For a few minutes, the family laughed together in a jovial manner as they typically did while gathering for a holiday. It was not to last, however, thanks to one ill-considered comment that Ned was destined to make.

"Yes, that's right!" the younger Ned stated as he spoke to Colin's grandfather. "I got that job at the Panther refinery!"

"Good for you, boy!" his grandad replied. "I done told you that Bill would hire you!"

"Uncle Ned, please don't say it…" the present day Colin muttered. But the past version of his older relative could not hear him, and things as already writ were not to be changed.

"Yeah, he did!" Ned mentioned with a tone of haughty pride. "That's more than he did for my black sheep of a bro here, right, Monty? Hah! Hah!"

Monty simply looked down with a glum expression and uttered something under his breath. "Fuck you, Ned."

"Say what, now?" Ned responded. "I'm kidding with you, man. You didn't have to be such a dick about it."

"That wasn't funny," Monty rejoined. "Now I have to hear your shit about being turned down, all because of some stupid mistakes I used to make when I was still in fucking high school. Something Bill wouldn't have even known about if we wasn't a friend of Dad. Any minute now Grandad is going to start on me about it…"

The younger Colin kept eating nervously as his mother spoke up next. "Come on now, you guys. This is Christmas, so let's not have this…"

30

"I'm not going to say anything!" Grandad hastily added. "Let's just go back to enjoying the dinner, okay?"

"Now we're all tense and shit because my little bro can't take a bit of ribbing," Ned continued against the advice of everyone present. "Like it's my fault that he used to be a little fucking thief."

Monty stood up so violently that he knocked over both his chair and his dinner plate of half-finished food.

"I'm outta here! I need to get away from this asshole brother of mine! All of you think he's so goddamned perfect! At least I'm not an asshole like him!"

"Monty, don't go!" Mr. Reynolds said. "You know Ned has a big mouth, and he didn't mean nothing by it."

"Yeah, you come back here and finish eating," Grandad agreed. "Ned is gonna apologize as soon as you sit back down."

"Fuck that," Monty remarked as he ran out the front door.

"Monty…!" Mrs. Reynolds yelled. She then turned to her brother. "Damn you, Ned!"

"Okay, okay, I'll go get him, and I'll tell him I'm sorry!" Ned shouted as he raced out after his younger sibling.

Ned pursued his brother for over three blocks before catching up to him. He grabbed the smaller man by his arms and held him in place. Colin and the Spirit easily kept pace with no need to actually move.

"Leave me the fuck alone, Ned!"

"No, you listen to me! I'm sorry, okay? I didn't mean to start shit! I'll talk to Bill; I'll get you a job at the refinery, alright? We'll build your rep back up again."

"I don't need your help with anything!" Monty shouted, now in tears as he unsuccessfully attempted to wrest himself from his larger brother's grip.

"Just listen to me, okay? Just for one fucking minute!"

That's when things took a truly dark turn. Out of the shadows behind them emerged a figure. It was none other than Santa Claus. Actually, it was only a local criminal wearing an outfit he had taken at gun point from a corner Salvation Army worker. When that ruse failed to bring in enough coin for the convict, he decided to take an even more proactive collection effort for himself.

"Excuse me, gentlemen," the colorfully garbed criminal said with his 9MM pointing at the two brothers. "I'm collecting for my favorite charity... myself. Now, hand it over."

"Seriously, man?" Ned replied. "Dressed as Santa Claus?"

"Do you expect me to ask you to sit on my fucking lap or something?" the convict remarked. "It's cold out here and I'm freezing my ass off, so just hand over your fucking money and let's be done with this!"

"Monty, give him the money," Ned insisted.

But the younger man was still very upset, and not at all acting rationally. "I can't believe this fucking night." He turned to the gun-wielding Santa. "Fuck you, too!"

Ned screamed in horror as the gun went off and his sibling fell to the snow-covered curb with a bleeding 2-inch hole in his throat. The gunman ran away, his garb and the holiday leaving an indelible image in the older sibling's head. Ned didn't return to the dinner that night but stayed put holding his dying younger brother while screaming apologies to him. That was where he was when the police and ambulance arrived minutes later, just far enough from the family home that they heard none of this.

Colin likewise fell to the ground crying. He had never been privy to exactly what happened to his Uncle Monty.

"Because of my age," he wept to the Spirit, "the family kept this from me. I didn't know Uncle Monty died for over a year. They told me he just ran away... because he was so pissed off. So, when they figured they had to tell me something, 'cause I would never see him again, they said he died from pneumonia while working in another state. I was told Ned never wanted to discuss it... so I kept mum about it."

The impact of what he had just learned hit Colin in the face like a metaphorical wrecking ball.

"I... didn't know. I didn't understand."

"But now you do," was the Spirit's only reply.

The Colin of the present continued crying alongside the Ned of the past until the cops and EMTs of that era arrived and the scene was replaced with blackness.

***

Colin opened his eyes to find himself in a vastly different environment. It looked like nothing less than a decrepit village from some dimly lit dystopian world combined with a nightmare version of Toyland, as twisted variants of every type of toy he had ever seen were strewn about.

To make matters even more horrifying, a number of these toys were moving about; some on wheels, and others on their feet. The more humanoid among them were jester-attired mannequins and those resembling oversized teddy bears. All of these had sinister visages with mouths opened to expose sharpened porcelain teeth.

He also became aware that he was standing next to a tall, brightly colored being that looked as if it hailed from a much more joyous world than wherever this was. Colin at first mistook this entity for Santa Claus, the real one this time, save for a few notable differences from the traditional American image of Kris Kringle. For instance, this being was much taller than Claus was supposed to be, with a bristling beard and bald head decorated with a wreath of holly. It was dressed in a simple green robe opened in the front to reveal a well-muscled torso. A rusty scabbard sans an actual sword completed the sartorial accoutrements of this being.

Colin's mouth dropped open. "Who are…?"

"You can call me the Ghost of Christmas Present," the Spirit said in a friendly but authoritative voice. "You have seen what your uncle experienced in the past to cause his displeasure with the holiday you hold dear. Now you can see where that has brought him, in the time you know as now."

"You mean… this is where the Krampus lives?"

"It is."

"My uncle is here?"

"He is."

"Jesus! Can we get him out?"

"I can only point you the way, show you what you face in the time of now. You and others must act on his behalf if you ever hope to extricate him from the clutches of the unholy fiend that makes this dismal land his home."

"Colin…?" came a weak, despondent voice that the young man quickly recognized.

"Uncle Ned! Is that you?" he replied in the voice's general direction.

"Help me, kid. Please."

Colin looked up to see that what he at first mistook for a huge heap of trash was actually an enormous wind-up vehicle with rust-covered parts. Chained to the front of it was Uncle Ned of the present, who looked beaten, bloody, and drained of will but not seriously injured. At the top of the vehicle's mast, chained in a lying down position with their feet opposite each other, were his friends Dack and Berry, who were likewise taken from the cabin Colin shared with his uncle. Those two barely moved and said nothing, each suffering from multiple injuries.

"Uncle Ned, I found you! I'll get you out of here!"

On hearing that, two of the humanoids surrounding the hodgepodge vehicle began rushing towards Colin.

"They can see and hear me too?"

"But of course," the Spirit confirmed. "Did you think only your uncle could? This is, after all, the *present.*"

Colin was thankful that the second Spirit, like the first, allowed him to keep his rifle. He had no time to grab any spare ammo when he rushed out of the cabin, so he realized that he had to use the bullets wisely.

As one of the walking toy jesters ran at him, Colin pulled the trigger, blowing the top of its seemingly plastic head off. A spurt of blackish ichor spewed from the "wound" and the being released a piercing shrill scream of seeming agony before falling on the dingy ground and going into spasms.

The other assailant, resembling a human fetishist known as a "furry," opened its mouth and released a roar that had an

34

uncomfortable resemblance to an actual bear. The monstrous teddy's bared teeth likewise looked authentically ursine. The nightmare iteration of a child's best friend had its torso blown out by Colin's next shot. A combo of what looked like stuffing and shattered ribs flew out the exit wound, and the impact dropped the screaming monstrosity on its back.

Colin was aware that he had about five shots left, and he meant to use them sparingly. That was when he suddenly noticed a whirring sound that he had heard before. The source was a pair of small, bright red toy fire trucks that had been set down on the ground by the remaining two mannequins. This was a threat used against him by the Krampus back at the cabin.

The twin mini-vehicles extended tubes from their front sections and began squirting twin streams of corrosive fluid at the intruder. Colin was expecting this move, however, and he swiftly backed away to avoid the liquid assault, recalling that their range was about four meters at most.

Not wanting to waste any more bullets than necessary he ran forward and smashed the first mobile toy to pieces with a strong blow from the butt of the rifle. The second one swiveled its turret to spew on its target in the direction he now stood. Colin swiftly countered this by kicking the truck over and reducing it to scrap metal with a second blow of the gun's hard wooden buttstock.

That was when he heard his uncle's voice again. "Colin, get me out of here…"

The young man pointed the rifle at the large vehicle, ready for whatever came next. He noticed, however, that the remaining two mannequins had released the fire trucks to distract him just long enough that they were able to get inside the front of the giant wind-up truck and drive it away. The bizarre automobile appeared to be steam operated as it released a series of whirrs and clicks and drove away at surprising speed, disappearing into the darkness of this putrid world's horizon.

The last thing Colin could hear other than the fast receding sounds made by the vehicle was his uncle's fading pleas for help.

"Uncle Ned! Noooo!"

"Do not waste effort with a pursuit, young sir," the Spirit said, now oddly looking and sounding much older than before, an indication that its current phase in linear time was almost up. "You shan't catch it."

"You said I could save my uncle!"

"I said that you can. And you yet *may*. But not this go round, I fear. My time grows short, and we must now depart"

"No, wait! You can't…!"

The Spirit seemed genuinely conciliatory and reproachful as it shook some sparkly dust from a glowing torch into Colin's face. This caused him to nod off and the dystopian scenery around them went black.

***

When Colin came to, he shook his head and rubbed his eyes to restore all sensation to himself. Upon looking around, his new locale seemed to again be that of Krampus's realm, only more enshrined in shadow, and somehow more… distant? Was that the word? That is the term which came to his mind, even if he only seemed to understand it on some subtle level. Everything appeared silent, with even the air about him being still.

That is when he turned to see a tall figure in a dark, cloaked garment that made him shudder in its eeriness. At first he thought it might be the Krampus himself, come to dispose of him once and for all. But that seemed wrong to him, as the Ghost of Christmas Present appeared benevolent, and would not transport him into the clutches of such a beast. Right?

Upon closer scrutiny of the being standing grimly and quietly before him, Colin realized that his hopeful conjecture was likely correct. It was not the Krampus. The absence of horns jutting from the cloaked head made that much clear. Hence, the figure could only be the third Spirit he was set to encounter.

"Are you… the Ghost of Christmas Future, I guess you would be called?" the young man asked with a hint of cautious trepidation.

The being gave no verbal answer, but simply pointed to the left with a spectral white hand.

"What?"

Colin looked in the direction the Spirit indicated to see a most startling display going on before him. It seemed that all was still in this version of the Krampus's land *until* the reaper-like entity pointed to direct his gaze there.

The scene appeared to be of a small but violent war, with the sounds being a mishmash of gunfire, animal-like growls, human screams, and the motorized clanging of vehicles. Several murky forms could be made out running around in the haze, and Colin squinted to make them out better. In the meantime, the Spirit simply stood still as a statue, continuing to point its index finger in the right direction.

As visual acuity and the specifics of the sounds became clearer, Colin swore he could see himself as he looked now, firing the rifle. He could hear the howls and grunts of the Krampus's toy-like minions and make out several varieties charging amongst the skirmish in spooky silhouette.

A massive form that resembled a hybrid of a man and a wolf could also be discerned in the midst of the skirmish. This being's lupine brow was covered with what appeared to be a black skullcap, and he slashed and punched at various foes attacking him. Two other male figures seemed to fight at his side, but it was too difficult for Colin to see them in any fine detail, and the faint sounds of their voices were not recognizable

At one point, he heard his own voice shout, "Hold on, Uncle Ned! We're coming!"

That moment was when he saw the highlighted figure of what could only be the Krampus walk onto the scene, something that the group of future outworlders could not fail to notice.

"Oh, shit..." Colin said in unintended tandem with his seemingly future self, the wolf-like man, and the other two accompanying them.

Then... the murky haze began congealing around the scene, and all started going blank again.

"Wait, what's happening? Is this my future? Who are those… others?"

The Spirit did not answer, however. To do so would be akin to setting too much that might occur in stone. Instead, it raised its hand and the black shroud that concealed the future scene became completely opaque.

Colin screamed in protest, but he was helpless against a Spirit of such power, one that was an apparent avatar of both Death itself and the merciless flow of time.

The scene was about to change again. It would not be something Colin was prepared for, but one that he needed to face as his quest continued.

TO BE CONCLUDED…

CHRISTMAS COMBAT

It was the return of the blustery winds that Colin Reynolds felt when he next regained his cogency. He looked around to see that he was back in the blizzard-ridden environment of the Maine wilderness that he called home. It had just slipped past midnight at this point, making it the most nightmarish Christmas that he, and most other people, had ever experienced.

His rifle was in hand, and he determined to make the most of the five shots it had left in its chamber. Not knowing what to expect he looked around only to see himself confronted by a tall figure partly concealed by the darkness of the hour and the snow-saturated winds. He pointed his piece at the entity, but it didn't flinch. This concerned the young man at first, until closer scrutiny revealed that the Ghost of Christmas Future was still present.

"Oh, it's you," he said. "But… why did you bring me back here? I can't help my Uncle Ned in the woods!"

As usual, the Spirit made no verbal response. Instead, it pointed to the wilderness directly behind him. Colin turned to see two smaller figures rush out of the darkness and into the snow-covered clearing where he stood. His weapon was aimed in their direction, and the two newcomers stood back. He could see that they carried rifles of their own.

"Whoa, whoa! Don't shoot, mister!" one of the two interlopers shouted.

It was the voice of a young boy, one that Colin recognized upon reflection, despite having only heard it a few times in the past.

"Are you… Dillon Lumpkin?" he asked.

"Yes! And you're Colin Reynolds, right?" Dillon queried.

"I am! And who is your friend here?"

"I'm not his friend, I'm his cousin," Gavin Lumpkin stated with an irritated tone.

"Okay, fine," Colin replied. "What are you two doing out here at night? There are some dangerous things out and about tonight."

"No shit, Sherlock!" Gavin rejoined. "Our other cousin Laurel and our two favorite uncles were just killed in front of us by this monster bitch!"

"Huh?"

"Gryla!" Dillon shouted. "She is some type of old lady that is actually a monster from Icelandic folklore! But she's real, and she has this big monster cat with her, that's also from folklore. We're not lying, Colin! You gotta believe us! Please…!"

"I do believe you," was the young adult's surprisingly affirmative response.

"You… do?"

"Yes. There's some strange seasonal energy converging on this location, and… my Uncle Ned and two of his friends were taken by the Krampus tonight."

"You mean… *he's* here too?" Dillon said through startled eyes.

"Yeah… he is."

"Oh, shit… that's wonderful," Gavin noted while covering his face in despair.

"And this guy is also here," Colin added while pointing to the Spirit, whom the boys at first overlooked due to it being cloaked in the shadows.

"Oh my god!" Gavin yelled while pointing his rifle at the Ghost of Christmas Future.

The Spirit remained as unconcerned as ever in the face of a firearm pointed in its direction.

"Is that… the Grim Reaper?" Dillon asked while shivering, and not entirely because of the cold wind.

"Sort of, but not actually," Colin said. "He's more like some spirit of Christmas representing the future. Like Charles Dickens wrote about."

"I don't know about any Charles Dickless," Gavin interjected, "but that Gryla bitch is hunting us down! She's gonna kill us! You gotta help us, Colin!"

40

"I'm not sure what I can do against something like that," Colin replied. "And the Krampus might still be out here tonight too, so…"

"It is not *that* wretch you need be concerned with," came a hoarse, accented lady's voice from the darkness within the surrounding greenery, "but the one who truly rules the winter."

The three of them turned to see the grotesque crone-like form of Gryla emerge from between the snow-coated trees. At her side was a snarling Yule Cat, ready to pounce as always.

"Oh… shit," Gavin whispered. "We're done. Do we go down fighting or something?"

"If I may ask, good sir," the winter ogress addressed Colin. "Have you received any new clothing as a gift for the Christmas season this year?"

"Um… no," he answered with his rifle pointed at the hag.

"Hee Hee. That is too bad," she responded while patting her monstrous feline. "That one is all yours, my precious kitty."

The Yule Cat raised her back and began slowly approaching her newly targeted prey with a hissing growl, as if determined to toy with him before pouncing. Colin aimed his rifle, hoping it would do the job.

"Colin!" Dillon yelled. "Can't you get that Ghost friend of yours to help out? We need him!"

"I don't know!" Colin replied. He quickly turned to the Spirit. "Help us if you can! Please!"

"What are *you* doing here?" Gryla queried to the Spirit once she noticed its presence. "You have no business to concern you here. Do not interfere with my rightful actions, or you will suffer my wrath as well. I rule the winter land, not you!"

But the Spirit looked as indifferent to Gryla's formidable threat as it did when a rifle was pointed at it. For this being represented forces that transcended the boundaries that the winter witch worked within and was equally empowered by the season. It also had a mission to see that Colin Reynolds and this new company he found survived to make certain contributions to the future.

Accordingly, the Spirit glided forward to intercept the Yule Cat before she could finally make spring on her intended prey. It then raised its ghostly hand and a hazy barrier seemed to prevent the vicious feline monstrosity from reaching her intended meal.

"Back away from my cat!" Gryla screeched as she raised her own bony hand.

The blowing winter winds seemed to condense and congeal around the Spirit. This enabled the Yule Cat to run through the weakened energy barricade towards her prey. However, the actions of the Spirit gave Colin time to properly aim his firearm. He released a shot, hitting the attacking feline in her left shoulder. A bloody wound appeared, and the supernatural animal screeched in agony. She was given pause but continued moving forward.

"Gavin, we gotta help Colin!" Dillon decreed. "Aim and fire at the witch!"

They both did so, and the lead projectiles caused Gryla distracting pain as they pierced her wrinkled flesh. She growled in rage and turned her attention to the two boys.

"Thank you for reminding me that my true quarry was still here," she spat. "Now, you will pay for disrespecting your auntie yet again this night."

She raised her arms in preparation of ripping the two boys to shreds. They aimed their weapons and prepared to fend her off as best they could.

***

In the meantime, Colin had four bullets left, and he hoped all of them would be enough to take the Yule Cat down for the count. He aimed, but before he had a chance to fire the feline leapt at him. The animal was suddenly halted in mid-air when a large, clawed hand unexpectedly grabbed her by the shaggy scruff of the neck while in mid-jump.

"No, this one is *mine*," declared the Krampus as he hurled the snarling Yule Cat at least a hundred feet away into the distant shrubbery.

"I knew you were still around here somewhere, you son of a bitch," Colin said as he re-directed his rifle sights to the Christmas monster. "Thank you for saving me from the cat, despite your selfish reason for doing it. Now, you let my fucking uncle and his friends go!"

"I shall not," the Krampus said. "Instead, I will take *you* to *them*, where you shall all remain for eternity." The creature pulled the sack he carried off his back and opened it. "Get in, or I shall have you pulled inside quite painfully. Your faith in the season is crushed, and you now belong in my domain."

"Bullshit!" Colin cried defiantly. "I won't let you make me lose my faith! There is good in the world and this season represents it! And the goodness is going to kick your ugly, grungy ass!"

"We shall see," was the monster's only reply as he shook his bag to release a sinister-looking toy soldier over five feet in height.

The seemingly synthetic man immediately raised a rifle to counter Colin's own.

"Get in the bag… or my soldier will drag you in with a sharp hook and chain," the Krampus warned.

***

As Gryla descended on the two boys, she suddenly found herself grasping the gnarled hands of… herself. The ogress then noticed that the Spirit had raised its hand, having stifled her by apparently summoning her own counterpart from a few seconds in the future!

"Pah!" she shouted. "Away with you, my other self!"

With that, her counterpart turned to frost and was absorbed into her body, thus eliminating that near-future timeline where she was used against her past incarnation.

"You think you have more tricks up your robed sleeve than a wise one of ancient lineage like me?" Gryla asked her foe rhetorically. "I shall freeze your ethereal form to the marrow!"

The Spirit merely raised both hands as if welcoming the primeval hag to make that move.

43

***

Before the large toy soldier could fire its bayonet hook into Colin, the mechanical man was deterred when the Yule Cat emerged from the thickets and pounced on it. The animal ripped the automaton's left arm out of its socket, causing it to drop its firearm. The feline monstrosity was not about to allow another to claim her chosen prey.

To counter the renewed threat of the Yule Cat, the Krampus growled in anger and opened his bag to release a big mechanical toy dog that looked as if it was constructed by a deranged kid with an erector set. This automated canine opened its hinged mouth to bare a set of razor-sharp metal teeth and growled through a speaker system of some sort that was located down its gullet. Krampus's mechanimal stood to bar the Yule Cat's path towards Colin. The feline met the challenge by attacking this new threat, and the two monstrous beasts fought and tore into each other ferociously.

This attracted the attention of Gryla, who was enraged to see yet another powerful interloper interfering with the rightful hunt of both her and that of her beloved cat.

"Krampus!" she shouted. "You have no business here any more than the Spirit of the Future does! Call that toy of yours off my cat, or there will be literal Hel to pay!"

"Gryla," the Krampus grumbled in retort. "My business with this one started before yours. You threaten me at your peril. Now, back away, call your animal off, and leave this one to me."

"Hsssssss… we shall see where the peril lies, you maggot-eating piece of cattle dung!"

The ogress was determined to make good on that threat by lunging at the Krampus. He met the attack, and the two powerful winter grotesqueries began pummeling and clawing at each other with furious abandon.

Gryla took the early advantage, punching her adversary in the face and cracking his fanged jaw. She then pounded him on his head, sending the being down to his knees. But the Krampus followed this up by slamming his horns into the winter witch's bloated paunch. This knocked her back several feet, and he followed up with two brutal slashes to her face that ripped her wrinkled skin from her skull like tissue paper.

"Graah! Now you done got me mad!" Gryla exclaimed as she rushed forward and belted the Krampus in his half-goat face with her gnarled fist. The impact sent him flying backwards, to slam into a high snowbank almost twenty feet away.

Several yards away, the two boys found themselves caught between a proverbial rock and a hard place.

"What the hell can we do?" Gavin asked his cousin. "Should we shoot the both of them while they fight? And what if that robot dog, or whatever the hell it is, doesn't beat the cat? Or, what if it does and then it comes after *us* next?"

Dillon responded by calling to their new ally. "Colin! What can we do? Is there anything else your Ghost friend can do for us?"

"I'm not sure – whoa!" he suddenly shouted as Gryla was tossed directly over his head, almost slamming into him in the process.

Then one of the Krampus's chains entwined around the Spirit, holding it fast despite the fact that the being was more spectral than physical.

This entity will not do anything to help you," the creature groused in his low, scratchy voice. "At least, *now* it won't."

As if answering a dare, the Spirit raised its arms as much as it could and whatever metal the Krampus's chain was composed of suddenly rusted and crumbled as if it had suddenly been aged thousands of years. The reaper-like being then turned to face the seasonal monster and again raised its hand, creating a barrier of force between it and the humans.

Krampus pounded on the field of mystical energy relentlessly, leaving the equivalent of "dents" on its glimmering surface but failing to break through. At least, for the moment.

"You will not... keep me from him!" the creature insisted. "He has lost what he once felt for Christmas, and that means he is mine to take. And I shall also claim those boys, if for no other reason than to slight that foolish Gryla!"

"You will do naught to vex me any further!" came the ogress's distinctive voice as she grabbed Krampus from behind and held him in a vice-like stranglehold. "I shall consume thee on the spot, despite the risk of indigestion that may bring me!"

With their two monstrous humanoid foes again distracted, and the Yule Cat still engaged in fierce combat with the canine automaton, the boys ran up to Colin.

"We need to do something while we have a minute!" Dillon said.

"I know that!" Colin replied. "There's only one thing I can think of since I don't want to rely on the Spirit here. There may be only so much he can do because of all the bullshit rules these beings have to follow. But we can try to pray to the spirit of Christmas."

"Say what?" Gavin muttered. "Are you shittin' me?"

"No shitting, kid!" Colin stated. "The energies around this place allowed the Krampus and Gryla to manifest here. But it let the Three Ghosts do the same thing, and they're not evil. The Christmas Force works both sides, I guess you could say. So, let's focus on the spirit of St. Nick and ask him for help!"

"Seriously, man?" was the irate boy's next response.

"Gavin, he might be right!" Dillon said. "We have to have faith! Maybe the Ghost here can help us with that. But we need to try!"

The three then glanced to see the Yule Cat on the verge of victory over her opponent as she had by now succeeded in ripping two of the toy canine's mechanical limbs from its body.

"Let's try it now!" Colin screamed.

The two boys took his hands without hesitation and began focusing their emotions into the most dedicated prayers they had ever mustered. They did so while gazing at the Spirit, hoping that it could somehow channel their impassioned benedictions to worlds beyond. The entity raised one hand as if precisely doing that.

While they did this, Gryla bit into the Krampus's shoulder, ripping out a big chunk of his hairy flesh. The monster howled as darkish blood flowed down his hirsute chest.

"You could really use some salt," the ogress said with a full mouth as she chewed her adversary's meat.

"Fah! You bitch!" the Krampus shouted as he pushed backwards with all his might and slammed Gryla into a heavy birch tree, causing her vice-like grip to slacken.

The monster then wrenched free of her completely.

"You gored me, and now I shall gore *you!*" he exclaimed while charging at his foe with his head down.

The creature's horns penetrated clear through Gryla's gut and halfway into the wood of the tree she was pinned against. His malformed cranium quickly became soaked in her blood.

"Raah! You play rough, but Auntie Gryla can play rougher still!"

"We shall see!" the Krampus replied as he turned his head to and fro to worsen the grisly laceration in his adversary's belly.

"Away from me, you fool!" the ogress bellowed as she kicked at her foe, sending him hurtling backwards, thus removing his horns from her paunch.

She then rubbed the painful bloody wounds on her tummy. "You... will... pay... for that!"

Several feet away, just as the Yule Cat finished off her foe by crumpling its metal head in her jaws like tinfoil, the three humans' invocations to the Christmas Spirit seemed to reach a crescendo.

Just as the feline fury fully destroyed her mechanical foe and turned her attentions back to her selected prey, what appeared to be a fissure in time and space opened before the praying threesome and the Spirit. Out of it stepped a personage that was familiar to virtually everyone on the planet in one guise or another.

"Ho! Ho! Ho!" the newest arrival laughed. "What have we here now? I believe someone called in a most compelling fashion." He then noticed the Ghost of Christmas Future standing before him. "Ah, so it would appear that you helped get the message to me."

"Are… you… shittin' me?" Gavin muttered. "Is that really… *him?"*

"It has to be," Colin answered with a smile, something he believed that he would never do again during the events of the past two hours.

"Yes…" Dillon said with a beam of his own.

The Yule Cat stopped and raised her hackles at the newcomer. This was not someone she wished to attack without strong consideration.

"I see that nuisance of a cat is here," Santa noted. "This does not bode well at all for the three people I see before me. The situation must be dealt with in due fashion."

The feline hissed like a cobra and charged at Colin, hoping to rip into him before either Claus or the Spirit could intervene. However, the red-cloaked new arrival raised his black-gloved hand and another fissure appeared, this one almost twenty feet above the snowy ground.

Out of that portal emerged a large flying male reindeer, who swooped down to intercept the attacking beast. The buck slammed into the Yule Cat with his mighty antlers, piercing her side and sending the animal sprawling across the ground for several yards.

The deer then landed beside Santa. "You never fail to arrive just in time when summoned, Blitzen," the jolly old dignitary said.

"Glad I could be of service," Blitzen replied, the animal's use of speech startling the three humans in his presence. "Then again, making good time is what we do best."

"Quite so," Santa agreed with a hearty laugh.

Blitzen then lowered his antlers, prepared for the Yule Cat's next assault.

"Shall we do this, cat?" the sentient deer asked. "Or, will you yield?"

The feline hissed ferociously and backed away slightly, clearly weighing her options carefully.

That was when the battling Krampus and Gryla ceased clawing and pounding at each other to notice the new threat which had just emerged onto the playing field.

"Hold, Krampus! *He* is here!" the ogress exclaimed.

The horned monster turned and saw that his rival had spoken the truth. "Grrrah. This is not good. As if that time Spirit were not trouble enough. We must put aside our quarrel and combine our efforts if we are to come out with anything this night. We can divide the spoils between us afterwards."

"I see… no other choice," the winter witch said with a disgruntled hiss.

The two then began at Santa and the Spirit in tandem.

"Colin!" Dillon yelled. "The monsters are coming at us!"

"I'll shoot the fuckers!" Gavin hollered as he pointed his rifle at the approaching threat.

"What you will do is both watch your language and step aside, young lad," Santa said. "You will let me handle this, for I fear your weapon is not sufficient to the task."

The Lord of the Season then turned to the Ghost of Christmas Future. "I must commandeer your presence to aid me in dealing with this menace as expeditiously as possible, to minimize the chance of a mortal casualty. We both serve the same higher force, and it permits me this authority under such circumstances."

The Spirit said nothing but offered no sign of defiance. It simply raised both hands in preparation.

"Blitzen, you keep the cat at bay. The Ghost and I shall deal with this twosome."

"No need to worry, sir," the reindeer replied. "This cat is as good as spayed if she goes for it."

Santa raised his own right hand, and the wintry winds congealed in front of him to form an enormous shield of ice several feet thick. Krampus slammed into it and his progress was momentarily halted as a result. The monster began angrily punching at the freeze barrier, determined to use his enormous strength to smash through the obstacle.

Gryla stopped several feet in front of the Spirit and upraised her knobby hands in a summoning stance. "Now you shall see who is the true mistress of winter."

Cold December energies suddenly manifested as ethereal bonds that surrounded the Spirit, holding it seemingly immobile.

"The force of time is embodied in the seasonal cycle, and I control the forces of the most powerful of the four!" the ogress cackled. "I will prove your superior!"

The Spirit appeared unable to break the bonds, but it didn't actually have to. Instead, it simply seemed to vanish as a portal opened behind it to release a counterpart from seconds in the future.

"Grrrr, I keep forgetting that time and space are connected like so," the witch griped. "Ah well, it is never too late in an immortal life to learn."

Krampus finally smashed through the last layer of Santa's ice shield, but this gave the quasi-deity ample time to make his next move. He summoned forth several of the sentient spirit globes that inhabit his North Polar pocket dimension through a portal. Next, he commanded them to merge with and animate a small battalion of snowmen that he created by willing the blowing snow to condense into forming their frozen bodies.

Upon gaining life the living men of snow simultaneously yelled "Happy Birthday!" and promptly pig piled onto the Krampus.

"Nothing like some winter team spirit, of the most literal sort," Santa remarked.

The snowmen pounded and struck the winter monster, but despite their numbers his own blows proved stronger. Within several minutes he shattered their icy bodies into tiny fragments. A group of displaced spirit globes left the destroyed forms and departed the scene at light speed.

"Hah! You cannot stop me, old fool!" Krampus boasted.

"Is that a challenge, my darkling counterpart?" the jolly immortal asked.

Krampus emptied a bunch of toys out of his sack, and the miniature legion charged at Santa. The red-garbed one snapped his gloved fingers and a sack of his own materialized from where he had it stored. He then dumped out a collection of his own toys, similar to the Krampus's but much brighter and colorful. These constructs were equally animated and rushed forth to counter his opponent's brigade. Both sides ripped each other to smithereens and effectively engaged in mutual neutralization.

"It would appear I need aid of a different sort," Santa said and again snapped his fingers.

Another, far larger fissure in time and space appeared. From it emerged a twenty-foot, ivory-furred yeti that roared through a mouth of sharp teeth.

The giant snow monster took Krampus by surprise and kicked him with as much force as the beast could muster, sending the dark entity through the air to land what appeared to be many miles distant.

"That would be the end of that, it seems," Santa noted.

"Did... did you see that?" Gavin asked Dillon.

"Yeah. Pretty badass, huh?" his cousin replied.

Colin still held his rifle at the ready, intending to put its final four bullets to use if required.

Gryla noticed the loss of her erstwhile ally and turned away from the Spirit. "I have an eternity to deal with the likes of you. But I have always delighted in slaughtering giants, including those which I had married."

The ogress ran behind the towering yeti, taking him by surprise much as he did the Krampus. She slammed her fist into the space behind the man-beast's knee, bending the leg and sending the furry monster to the ground with a loud crash. Gryla then jumped on his massive torso and grabbed the top and bottom of his maw, pulling them open and breaking the creature's jaw. She smiled as her gown was stained by blood spurting from the tissue formerly connecting the yeti's mandible bones.

"Shit!" Gavin yelled.

"Fire on that bitch!" Colin commanded.

He and the two boys did exactly that, riddling the winter witch with bullets. The three-sided fusillade caught her unawares and sent her off the injured yeti.

"I must spirit you away so you can be tended to by my medic elves," Santa said as he snapped his fingers and the giant fell into a dimensional fissure created directly under his fallen form. "Thank you for your service and what it cost you. That shall be remembered."

Gryla then jumped to her feet, not at all bothered by the several bleeding puncture wounds on her aged but powerful form.

"Raahh! I will unleash the full frozen fury of Niflheim upon you, Kringle!"

She raised her arms and directed gale force winds of frigid intensity at her scarlet-attired opponent.

"It will avail you naught," Santa stoically retorted as he snapped his fingers and summoned a tornado-sized whirlwind of his own.

He then turned to the Spirit. "Combine your force with my own… time and temperature together."

The Ghost of Christmas Future did as bade, raising its arms and directing a mass of shimmering blue energy to surround Santa's whirlwind. This vortex smashed through the wave of whiteness sent by Gryla and enveloped the ogress in short order.

She screamed in protest, uttering vile obscenities in a language lost to the ages as the cyclonic maelstrom of freezing wind and snow condensed about her. After several minutes it ceased its fury to reveal a massive, tube- shaped pillar of ice, almost a quarter of a mile thick. Suspended in the center was an unmoving Gryla.

"That will do for now," Santa lamented.

Meanwhile, Blitzen continued to stand his ground and slam his antlers into the Yule Cat, managing thus far to block her attempts to slice his throat open with her claws. As soon as the feline saw her mistress trapped in the ice, however, the animal hissed and backed down. She retreated with great speed into the darkness of the forest, realizing that she would not be feeding again on this particular holiday cycle.

"Yeah, you better run," was Blitzen's concluding comment.

***

The three humans ran to Santa's side.

"Is… is it over? Are they both gone?"

"For the nonce," the Christmas King replied. "But they are ancient powers connected to forces that rival though never exceed those which empower me. Each year I endeavor to oppose their depredations, but I am unable to do so in every single instance. The darkness can always be countered, but never fully eradicated until humanity at large collectively makes the choice to create a better way for itself. In the meantime, I have others of your race fighting for the greater good, from my mortal Helpers to the agents of the Aquarian Alliance."

"I've heard of that on the Internet, when I get service here," Dillon said. "So, that's real too. Sort of like a good version of the Illuminati, or something like that?"

"Yes, something like that, lad," Santa concurred. "After what you boys have dealt with today, it would be my honor if you two became my newest recruits. I am sorry for the losses you suffered this day, but you could avenge them and all that is good in this world by becoming soldiers for the forces of light."

"We can join the Aquarian Alliance?" Gavin asked. "That's really bitchin'! I'm in!"

"You need to work on that language, young man," Santa said, "but rougher edges than your own have served me well as my agents. I am proud to have you as the latest of that august body."

"But…" Colin interjected. "Maybe the boys here want to join your, um, Alliance, to avenge the loss of their family to these monsters. But me… I just want to rescue my uncle, and maybe his friends too if I can. They're still alive, and the Krampus has them. I won't rest until I get them out of his realm. I've been there and it's a horrible place, so I can't just leave them there. Can you help me?"

"I can, but I fear that I cannot act as directly as you wish," Santa explained. "There are rules governing such things, and times when my power is just not sufficient. Krampus resides in a world of magic, and venturing there now, so close to sunrise, would leave you trapped in that world of deviltry for the entire year along with your uncle and his friends.

"But I will give you a contact card, and I want you to use that to locate a man named Mike Nero, one who is a wolf in my fold but in a beneficial way. He is an agent of the Aquarian Alliance, and in turn runs yet another organization, one who will surely help you rescue your uncle."

Santa handed him the card with the information on it, which was printed in a bright red, elaborately embossed font.

"And you say this Nero guy will help?" Colin asked.

"He will help," the scarlet-garbed personage replied, "as will others among his Knights, especially once you tell him that Kris Kringle sent you. However, it will require an entire year for you to locate him, and you can next enter the Krampus's realm on the following Christmas season."

Colin winced. "That long? I want to get my uncle out now!"

"You must be patient, as this quest of yours will unfold as it must. I wish you and the allies you will meet in this task well. In the meantime, I must now take my leave, along with the Ghost and my friend Blitzen. I shall see that you are sent into the city of London, Maine, and there you will begin your journey."

"But what about us?" Dillon inquired. "Are we safe from that witch now?"

"For the moment, lad," was Santa's answer. "For now, you and your cousin shall travel with me. You will soon be reunited with your family."

Claus snapped his fingers before the young man could say another word. A fissure opened and he, the two boys, and the reindeer vanished into it.

That left only the Spirit, who raised its ethereal hand a final time to again shroud Colin in a field of darkness. His next moment of cogent awareness found him in the middle of the city where he grew up, just as Santa promised. There was no blizzard conditions there, just an inch of snow on the ground and slush in the city streets. Colin was now left to his own devices to contact a certain individual despite having only a name to go by.

It would indeed take him a year, as he was told, but what a year it would be. And he was determined to spend that time gathering whatever aid he needed to rescue his uncle when the next Christmas season came about.

END

Colin Reynolds shall return, and his mission will conclude, the following Christmas in *Boogey Knights: Yuletide Horrors*. Dillon and Gavin Lumpkin will also be back, but where and when must remain a mystery for now.

BONUS SECTION

NERO: A HOLIDAY HAUNTING

Note: This short story occurs during *Nero Book 2: The Mummy Strikes* but is not connected to that novel's main sequence of events.

Buffalo, New York, Christmas Eve circa 1981

It was easy enough to catch the spoor of Ramus Edwards as he trekked down West Avenue after 7 PM. He walked in the street to avoid the snow and slush that covered the sidewalk and was carrying some type of bag with him, but I couldn't possibly care less what its contents were. I simply wanted *him*, or more specifically, to rip into his flesh and shed a lot of his blood. I wanted to hurt him for the occasions he hurt me, in my vulnerable human form, when Iwas weaker than him. He often did this alongside the great neighborhood bully Paulie Dano, who had also been on my target list until I recently marked him off... after I had marked him *up,* if you get my drift.

I received an early gift this holiday season when I happened to pick up Ramus' scent soon after going out and about. It was easy enough since I had gotten a good whiff of his entire crew in human form a few days ago. They intercepted me and a friend minding our own business and harassed us inside a coffee shop. The others were taken care of in bloody fashion later that evening, but Ramus was not with them when I – with some unexpected help – hunted them down soon afterwards.

Now, as then, I was in wolfen form, and I was getting closer and closer to Ramus on this freezing December night. Swift and silent, I kept mostly out of sight by dashing between and behind large bundles of snow and parked vehicles. I needed to be more careful than usual, because despite the heavy jacket and thick denim jeans he was wearing, I knew that the biting cold may have caused him to be more alert than usual.

Still, in animal form my stealth is off the charts, as only once did the doomed asshole look behind his shoulder after he thought he heard something. He did, of course, but I had darted behind a towering snowbank close to Holy Apostate Church before he was able to catch sight of my huge and terrifying form. I could already taste his blood in my gullet and the thrill of revenge as I moved onto the sidewalk and picked up speed, as he would be unable to see me behind the bulky mounds of compacted snow.

It was then that I felt what I can only describe as a "tugging" force coming from the big, dark, and seemingly deserted lot that was part of the Holy Apostate Church and connected schoolyard. I attended middle school there, and it was a place where I received many of the traumas that led me to voluntarily take on the power of the lycanthrope in shamanistic fashion when the remarkable opportunity presented itself. It was power I took on to seek retribution for the monster that the society I was born into had made me want to become.

This large Romanesque Catholic church and the buildings down the street from it, the latter by now a part of the small private Denville College, once harbored an insane asylum and a notorious orphanage. Those institutions were the source of many abuses towards their respective residents so many decades in the past and are responsible for much of the hauntings and negative mystical energies that to this day pervades the surrounding neighborhoods.

For some reason, though, this tugging sensation did not feel particularly malevolent. It was nigh-irresistible, however, and the mystical energies that powered my lupine form caused me to feel like an iron filament caught in the attraction field of a powerful magnet. After a few seconds, I decided not to attempt resisting any longer, and to allow it to lead me into the darkened, snow-filled school courtyard. I further decided that my impending revenge on Ramus could keep for now; he would be easy enough to locate another night.

I rushed into the schoolyard on all fours, my shaggy grayish fur blowing about in the freezing wind. I quickly detected something, not a true physical scent, but some form of sensation that the word "scent" is the closest I can come to describing it. It was as if I were detecting it on a psychic, not olfactory, level.

I ran and turned the corner of the school building into the courtyard to find myself confronted by a small misty form that seemed to congeal out of a whirling vortex of blowing snow. To my wolfen eyes, I saw what appeared to be the figure of a little girl, no older than eight years of age, emerge from the misty field of whiteness. Even in my powerful lupine form I was rather startled, as she seemed to be dressed in nothing but a thin, sleeveless white nightgown that was hardly adequate protection from the type of weather she was walking about in.

Even more strangely, though she did seem to be slightly shivering, it appeared to be more akin to some type of reflex action, as she didn't appear to be oppressively cold and on the verge of all-over frostbite as she should have been. No misty freezing air wafted from her mouth via exhalations that one expected to see and experience in such weather.

The girl had long, wavy brown hair, unusually alabaster-toned skin, and large hazel eyes that glared at me with great curiosity rather than the terror I expected. She wore no shoes and walked over the snow without experiencing the "burning" freeze on her bare soles that she should have. Her entire form – skin, hair, eyes, and clothing – seemed to have an ashen caste to them, as if her figure were tinted with the dreary sheen one sees on people appearing on a black and white television screen.

She stepped out of the whirling whiteness embedded against the darkness of the night a mere few feet from me. Being weary of this apparition, I bared the teeth in my muzzle and snarled at her. The girl phantom's only reaction was for her large eyes to open a bit wider. Then, she spoke to me in a soft, sweet, but slightly "echoey" voice.

"You're a big dog," she said. "Will you be my dog? I lost my best friend Gilmont, and I'm alone-ely."

"I wouldn't make... a good dog," I replied in my gruff lupine voice, forming the words through a half-human larynx with some effort. "I'm not housebroken. I'd... shit all over the floor."

The small apparition giggled pleasantly. "It's okay. I'd clean it up. So, will you be my dog?"

"I'm... not a dog. I'm a werewolf. See?"

I stood up on two legs, rising over her by several feet. "I'm not...a pet. I'm a monster. You... should go back to... wherever you came from."

She simply looked up at me with a half-smile and an expression of mild awe.

"Oh, whoo! I'd could have my own werewolf! The other kids would be jealous! But not so much as long as I let them pet you and feed you sometimes. Do you like left over beef jerky and celery sticks?"

Geez. I rolled my bright yellow eyes, but I couldn't help feeling sorry for this girl, and whoever she had been.

"So, I see you are still capable of tender feelings," came an even more echo-like voice from behind me. "Aren't you, Mike Nero?"

I turned and snarled, startled that this new apparition could identify me. When I saw the new phantom interloper, it was obviously more than just your average ghost. It was short in stature, had a distinct glow about its head, long white hair the same hue as the snow around me, and wearing a long white robe. It also carried some funky looking metal hat in its hand. The oddest thing about this spectre was that I couldn't easily distinguish its gender, a matter not helped by its voice, whose tone made it equally difficult to determine a sex.

Of course, I should have recognized this particular ghost immediately, as it was one I had read about before. I just never expected to actually meet this being, but in retrospect I should not be surprised that I did.

"I am the Ghost of Christmas Past," the spectre told me. "And I see your path on this fine white Christmas Eve has crossed that of little Clara."

"Lookee there!" the ethereal little girl exclaimed with excitement. "Must be someone new at the orphanage! Mr. Robe, will you let me keep the werewolf doggie? I think I'll call him Rex!"

Jesus.

"No! Don't you... dare call me that," I retorted.

Clara seemed to think for a few seconds. "Then how 'bout Esther? 'Cause you might be a girl werewolf."

"Grrrr..."

"Never you mind the temper, young Mike," the Ghost said firmly. "The fact that Clara's energies brought you to her as she manifested here is a strong indication that you are the one who can help her find peace. If you so choose, of course."

"How do you... know me?" I queried as I stood over the somewhat diminutive Ghost of Christmas Past like a titanic bipedal canine.

"I know all I need to know about those in your circumstances on this particular night," it replied.

"So, you have access... to Akashic Records," I huffed.

"Yes, that too," the Ghost admitted in non-committal fashion.

"Are you... male or female?"

"I have been perceived as either by different people whom I have encountered, and sometimes differently by those who have shared the same famous incident that made it into publication on your side of the veil. The nature of my gender, and why I am perceived in so ambivalent a fashion by different souls, is not important to the matter at hand, however."

"Why... are you here, then?" I asked, struggling to keep my animal aspect from taking over in a pique of anger and frustration.

"In short, I am here because Clara manifested this night, which so happened to be an evening that you were in the correct vicinity to sense her subconscious pleas for help and company."

"She appears here... every Christmas Eve?"

"I see this place a lot," Clara interjected. "The winter is always here. But I can't find Gilmont. He is my bestest friend, and I won't go away without him. He was all I had when things were bad. Now things are just quiet... and lonely."

I went back down on all fours and stood calmly as Clara's wispy hand reached out and touched my canine nose. I instinctively sniffed, but detected nothing like a human scent; instead, I detected a thin fragrance somewhat reminiscent of a bouquet of carnations.

"To answer your previous question, Mike Nero," the Ghost continued, "she has indeed appeared here each and every Christmas Eve since she died. Her spirit, however, became trapped here, as others have and most are prone to do if they experience unusual, traumatic, or violent endings to their story in such a 'charged' area. That is her Christmas Past, and why it attracted my attention when you two came together by chance... or, perhaps the will of some deities, possibly Sir Kringle himself. One can never be certain, not even an entity such as myself.

"However, let me note that the power of the lycanthrope is good for more than the selfish, bloody instrument of vengeance you have chosen it for. Beings such as you can also serve as defenders of the Earth. Or, in other cases, as useful guides to others on difficult journeys. And it is in the capacity of these latter two things that you have the choice to provide aid to Clara this night."

"I... don't know..." was all I could say.

"First, Mike Nero, please observe a Christmas past I am about to show you. Not yours, but that of Clara's."

The Ghost waved its wispy robed arm and suddenly the three of us were surrounded by a field of mist. In less time than it takes to describe it that mist had parted, and we were all somewhere else. It was a dismal corridor inside some type of building lit by old-fashioned lights. A few kids sat within the hallway, leaning back against doorways while arguing over access to the few toys they collectively had.

"This is the place!" Clara shouted as etheric tears poured out of her large oblong eyes. "This is where me and Gilmont lived before…"

I stepped back and suppressed the urge to snarl as I saw an older woman in a bluish uniform and severe bun who was obviously one of the staff appear.

"Do not fret, the three of us are invisible and inaudible," the Ghost explained.

"Clara!" we heard the staff lady shout. "What did I tell you about playing with the other kids when you are sick? You can spread whatever you have to them!"

The other kids moved away from Clara.

"I'm sorry," the little girl said. "I don't feel good, and I don't wanna be alone 'cause I'm scared. But it's alright if just Gilmont stays with me."

"You misunderstand, Clara!" the lady said. "You've been bad, and you need to keep away from the other kids until you're better. You have to go into the sick room, okay?"

"No! I don't like it in there! It's lonely!"

"I'm afraid you have to go!" the staff member insisted. "Come with me now!"

Clara struggled to no avail as the tall women grabbed the girl's wrist and pulled her into the sick room, where kids would go for temporary quarantine if ill. She then shut the door and locked it.

"Please let me out! I won't be bad again!" Clara screamed through pouring tears. "I'll just stay with Gilmont! That's all! Please!"

I turned to see the spectre of Clara I had interacted with crying along with this holographic vision of her past self. "No… I don't want to see this again… it's supposed to be over."

As I turned my attention back to the 3-D trip down the little girl's personal memory lane, I saw that Clara of the past continued shouting for a while, still proclaiming that she didn't feel good and didn't want to be alone. Eventually, I saw her get too weak to continue, and she just… stopped. Within seconds, the three of us were back in the present outside the freezing dark courtyard of Holy Apostate School.

Clara's wraith was covering her ethereal eyes and still crying. I felt as if would shed a tear too.

"What... happened then?" I asked, despite already knowing.

"I just found myself walking around," Clara said as she took her hands from her face. She was still shedding tears, but her eyes and face never got red or swollen. "Looking for Gilmont, so I can leave. I won't go without him, just like I know he stayed here just for me."

"So, this... Gilmont must be another ghost who is still stuck in that building," I surmised aloud. "Or, maybe he was one of the other kids, or a dog she once had?"

"Yes, something of that nature," the Ghost confirmed. "Because of the rules governing my appearances on this night to different individuals for different reasons related to their Christmas Past, I cannot show her the way directly. All I can do is show her past plight to a potential Samaritan and hope you will choose to help her."

"So, I... don't have to help," I said.

The Ghost sighed. "No, it would be pointless to your spiritual growth and opportunity for penance if I used my power to force you. I can only give you this offer after showing you Clara's travails and hope that you make the right choice, which to take a detour from the thorny path you have chosen, one that is no one's fault but your own. Do you wish to ignore this poor girl's plight and continue on the mission you originally planned for tonight? Or, will you at least temporarily step off the path, just this one special night, to help a lost soul in need?"

I thought about it, and quickly decided. "What she went through... same as what I did. What made me a monster... led to her becoming a ghost. I'll... help."

The ephemeral light around the head of the Ghost seemed to brighten for just a second, as if to highlight a smile from the being.

"This is a good start, young Mike Nero," the Ghost said. "But only a start, as much more work will be required to make a full redemption in the future… but that is then, not now. We must focus on the now that is related to Clara's past."

"How do I find this… friend of hers?" I asked, with the frustration causing the mane-like plume of fur adorning my upper back to stand up.

"That is not difficult, young Mike," the Ghost replied. "In your wolfen form, you have tracking abilities beyond that the mere animal-like detection of a lingering physical scent. You need simply concentrate on little Clara, focus on the psychic spoor that her dear friend Gilmont left upon her trapped etheric shell, and follow it as you would a true physical trail."

"So… wait," I said. "Is this… Gilmont actually flesh and blood? Maybe still alive… in that place? Can't be a dog or cat then. Maybe friendly staff member… some father figure type… maybe now very old, on verge of dying, but somehow… still there?"

"I can tell you no more, young Mike Nero," the Ghost said. "You must have the ecto-trail now, and you must make haste! Guide Clara to her friend so she will be emotionally amenable to leaving this plane and going to a better place… with her dear Gilmont."

This would make sense if that Gilmont is some old dude who was still alive, but about ready to croak If so, I would need to get Clara there fast. And… she deserves to be happy.

With a sudden puff of milky ectoplasmic mist, the Ghost of Christmas Past vanished. It was now just Clara and I, a werewolf saddled with a little ghost.

"Is what the robe person said the truth?" Clara asked me with wide open eyes. "Are you gonna take me to find Gilmont?"

"Yes," I replied. "You deserve… to be happy, Clara. Not like… me. Let's go find your friend."

As the Ghost had told me, it was not hard to follow that psychic trail. I was using my nose, and somehow following the "scent" on a whole other level. That was the only way I could find a possibly physical dude whom I never got the chance to sniff before. And as a phantom, Clara was unable to provide me with any physical object that had his scent on it.

As it turned out, the apartment building that used to hold part of the orphanage was just a few blocks away. I ran there on all fours at a quick pace, and Clara's ethereal form enabled her to float about just behind me, never losing track or in danger of being left behind.

"This is fun!" she said. "I wish you were my dog! We could play chase all the time! If ya don't like Esther, I think I would call you… Seymour!"

Geez. I feel like a character on one of those cartoons I watch every Saturday morning.

I did my best to ignore her echoey vocalizing for the few minutes it took me to reach the right building. It was old and decrepit and now seemed to be abandoned. That didn't mean it wasn't inhabited by someone, of course, as the trail totally led here.

"We have to… go inside," I told her.

My powerful form easily smashed the front door in, and the old wood splintered into numerous jagged pieces.

"Be careful… don't cut yourself on…" *Shit. She's intangible. She can't cut herself on the wood.* "Never mind."

The trail then led me up a flight of stairs, the ancient rickety steps almost collapsing under my 500 lbs. of weight.

"Be careful, these steps…"

Shit! I almost did it again. She'll just float above them if they collapse, you dickhead!

"Never mind. Just… follow."

Luckily, the staircase held up just enough so I could reach the third floor, where I was able to sense the presence of Clara's friend. He was in one of the rooms on the opposite side of the corridor. It didn't look good for his safety, however, because I now caught the scent of at least three other individuals, all of whom were also alive.

I growled reflexively, and one of the doors opened. Out of it came a youngish-looking man wearing the distinctive outfit of the

Red Dragon street gang. It just figured that Clara's friend had to be sequestered in the same abandoned building this gang had chosen to smuggle and sell narcotics from.

"Holy fuck!" the gangbanger yelled. "I think it's the West Side Wolfman! And he's got some kind of little weird-ass *chica* with him!"

"You gotta be shittin' me, man!" came a second voice as another guy ran out of the room. "Oh, fuckin' a, man! Terrace, we got trouble out here, man! Burn the stash if you gotta!"

I then growled a challenge and stood on two legs to look more intimidating. The first guy pulled out a pistol, and the other one went for a piece in a holster hidden inside his open red jacket as soon as he laid eyes on me.

Shit! Not more guns! I hate being shot!

Having no time to waste I charged at the two men as fast as I could move on two legs. I was luckily able to remember this time that my companion couldn't be hurt by anything those gangbangers brought to bear.

I slammed into both at once just as the first man fired a shot, but before the second one could fully draw his piece. The lead bullet simply grazed my left shoulder, which stung like Hel but caused no serious damage. Thankfully, the projectile didn't bury itself into my flesh like that incident two weeks ago with a different gang. I slammed both dudes on the floor and ripped into them savagely, my claws tearing huge gashes across the chest of one and my teeth crunching down on and removing four fingers of the other's gun hand.

They screamed in agony, their blood added to the scarlet color of their jackets, and my hunting urge was close to satisfied. Both men quickly passed out... but there was another, some guy named Terrace, who was still in the room.

How could Clara's friend be mixed up with these guys? Please don't tell me he's some really old geezer who is nowhere near as nice as Clara thought he was. If I have to rip into him too...

"Wow! My doggie bites!" Clara stated after she saw the carnage I carried out. "But that room down there… I live in it! But not anymore, I think! But Gilmont is still in there. I can feel it!"

That was when my keen nose caught a whiff of smoke. The last gang member was following the order to set the stash of narcotics on fire, willing to burn it all rather than let it fall into the hands of the police or some neighborhood hobos. And he was willing to risk burning down the whole building, himself, and his two friends – not to mention Clara's friend – along with it.

"No! That asshole man is not gonna hurt Gilmont!" Clara screamed as she ran into the room, easily passing through part of the door to do so.

"What the hell…?" I heard the thug shout as he saw Clara's ethereal form rush towards him.

I quickly entered the room to see Clara focus all her emotional energy into tossing a discarded empty beer bottle at Terrace's head. It hit him on the side of the skull, leaving a nasty gash. He fired at her with his piece, but the bullet simply passed right through her.

"Shooting at people is bad!"

You won't see me disagreeing with her, since I hate getting shot.

She then pointed her right arm and caused a coat rack to become airborne and slam into the gangbanger's lower gut like a martial artist's bo staff. He fell to the hard wood floor screaming God's name and probably his mother's too.

I struck him on the head with my closed fist, sending him into unconsciousness. At the same time, Clara caused the burning suitcase of narcotics to fly around the room at such speed that the fire was soon whisked out. As my occult studies had already shown me, the majority of ghosts lack the energy and sheer force of will required to wreak telekinetic and psychic havoc at the severity level I had just witnessed. But it seemed the extent of Clara's devotion to her long-lost friend, combined with the mystical forces inherent in this haunted neighborhood, had given her all the energy she needed to cut loose and bust some gangbanger ass.

Also, it was Christmas Eve.

"They are all… down," I said to her. "You did good, Clara."

"And you're a good doggy, Seymour!" she replied. Then she pointed to the closed door on the far side of the corridor. "That's… where I live. Or useta' live. Gilmont is still there."

"Let's… get him."

I didn't want to terrify whoever that guy was, but I realized that he must have heard the ruckus that went on just down the hall. So, I broke the rusted lock with a single hard push of my furry hand that sent the door flying open. I smelled nothing in there except for the dankness of the trapped air and my eyes didn't even detect the heat signature of a mouse.

So, where is…?

"Gilmont!" Clara yelled with excitement as she ran into a corner of the room.

Laying there amidst a pile of empty potato chip bags and candy wrappers was a beaten but still intact teddy bear. Her emotional energy still keeping her ethereal form strong, Clara walked up to the stuffed animal and tenderly picked it up, snuggling it in her misty arms like a baby.

"Thank you so much for helping me find Gilmont," Clara said as she walked up to me with the teddy bear in her arms. "Can I pet you?"

Seriously? Seriously?

"Do not fret, young Mike Nero," I heard the voice of the Ghost of Christmas Past say from the same corner Clara had retrieved Gilmont. "That faux animal meant much to her when she was alive. He comforted her during very trying days at that orphanage, and he was all she had the night she died of an unknown illness in this very room. What your culture refers to as 'stuffed animals' often serve as important totems, serving the function of friend, companion, and guardian to children and sometimes even people of greater age when they have no one else. These totems therefore become imbued with emotional and spiritual energy. I am aware

70

that several of them served you in such capacities during your own troubled childhood."

"Does this mean…?"

"Yes," the Ghost answered. "Now that you found her beloved friend, she is willing to leave for a better world beyond and I was able to manifest again as per the rules to help guide her there."

My lupine muzzle was unable to form either a proper smile or frown, and I'm not sure which I would have naturally had as my expression if I were in human form. And it was just as well.

"I… understand. Good luck, Clara."

"You're such a good werewoof! I wish I could take you where me and Gilmont are gonna go with the robe man now. Thank you much, Seymour!"

"Grrr… I wish you wouldn't call me that."

"Oh, did you like Rex or Esther better?"

"No! You can just call me… Mike."

"Oh, okay. Why did ya not just tell me that Mike?"

Geez.

"Bye bye, Mike! Gilmont says 'bye' too! We love you bunches!"

"Thank you, young mister," the Ghost of Christmas Past said as it took Clara's hand and guided her into a portal that emitted a very bright luminescence. "There is… hope for thee yet, my friend.

"And if you will, please do consider refraining from hunting young Ramus this night. The bag you saw him carrying contained a gift he saved up much allowance money to purchase for a little cousin who is ill and loves him greatly. I understand he has been vile to you, but others love him rather than hate him. If you choose not to be permanently merciful to that boy, then do at least consider allowing him and his family to have this night and tomorrow together. Merry Christmas to you."

"Bye…" I replied, waving to the Ghost and Clara as they stepped into the portal, which collapsed into nothing with a light whooshing sound.

I then stepped over the still unconscious and bleeding bodies of the two gang members sprawled in the hallway with the rest of the refuse and promptly left the building. I refrained from hunting Ramus or anyone else that night, deciding to return home with a determination to enjoy Christmas as much as I could.

END

CULMULUS25 AND THE CRANK: A Santa Claus Tale

Out of the altocumulus clouds in the night sky, a blazing green fireball shot down to Earth. The sparking, burning object crashed into a cornfield in rural Wisconsin. Muddy ground exploded, the remnants of the season's yield mixed in with the wet chunks of dirt that scattered all around. Seemingly unfazed by the impact, the thing from the sky continued to burn in the crater it had created, its lime-colored flames rippling across its surface like water.

After several minutes, the fire started dying, slowly dwindling until it snuffed itself out completely. What remained was a metallic green object, looking like the very fruit it was the hue of. Only the size of a large dog. A very rotund canine.

Suddenly it broke apart, cracking and whirring in a hiss of steam and red lights that illuminated the small divot it had put into the earth. The pieces of it moved apart, connected by hinges and connecting pieces that looked like they were made of muscle tissue instead of metal. From out of the glowing red openings where the sectional pieces had been, tendrils looking like twisted steel wool strips snaked out and sought *something, anything.*

Instead, they only found the dirt wall of the hole it was in. Undeterred, the strange thing from space transformed its tendrils into jagged appendages, complete with knees. The odd ribbons twisted and combined into four functional limbs made for locomotion, finished by the tips shaping into tiny, clawed toes at the ends.

The uncanny entity scrambled up the crater's slope, mud spitting out from between its imitation toes. Upon reaching the top, it stopped, hanging below ground level. From out of the blood-colored spaces within, two long stalks with spherical ends crept out and peered over the edge of the divot. Glowing red eyes with green pupils popped open at the end of each orbed extension. They blinked twice at the scene in front of them.

A small herd of Earthican herbivores and the sleigh they were chained up to were being fed individually by a large native denizen dressed in a suit redder than its internal processes. White fur, long and bushy, dangled from his face only. Strange a creature would not grow fur everywhere for warmth. It then heard the robed Earthican curse at no one in particular as soon as he had finished taking care of his livestock.

Suddenly, the first animal's nose lit up like an orb of red light, glowing with an intensity that cut through the dark like a guiding light.

"I know, my friend, but we ran out of juice because there's no snow here!" the large biped said. "This is Wisconsin! In December! No snow is practically blasphemy!"

The weird thing watching considered its payload. It belayed its decision, however, choosing to eavesdrop a little while longer.

Glowing fiercely, the red nose on the antlered animal leading the line blinked rapidly in a flash of quick bursts and longer, drawn out ones.

"Yes, I am aware that it's probably not going to snow tonight," he continued, "thanks for your observation, Lightbulb Face."

Lightbulb Face snorted and stomped his feet in protest to the name. The green visitor considered for the first time its understanding of the information coming out of the crimson uniformed guy's words, or even the fact that they were called "words." Suddenly, it was hit with a jolt out of nowhere, green electricity crawling across its form. It knew what it could do to save Santa Claus on this Christmas Eve on the Planet Earth. It knew who it was and why it was here.

Everything retracted back into the lime-colored craft, and it rolled back down to the bottom of the indentation it had created. It then jumped right back up into the sky on small propulsion jets spurting out of hole in the bottom of the thing. Hovering in place for a second, another opening began up on the exterior surface, a retinal camera lens focusing on the objects of interest it now knew it was there to help.

Floating toward him and his driving force slowly, CUMULUS25 considered its first action in its short lifetime, something meant to convince this fat human and his reindeer that he was a friend. The large humanoid looked up and spied the floating machine and smiled. "CUMULUS! My friend, am I glad to see you!"

C25 beeped affirmatively and took a position in the air ten feet out from Santa. It warbled and trilled almost organically and then went silent, waiting for a response. The bearded man cocked an eyebrow quizzically at him.

"Am I supposed to understand that?" he asked.

Almost sounding like laughter, C25 went crazy with sound for a second or two, then shut up and opened a small port atop its stippled, green exterior. A small ovular surface popped out at him, and a video began playing, prompting him to venture closer. What he saw when he got there made his face light up.

"You would do that for me?" he queried.

The viewscreen disappeared back into the shell and C25 blasted up into the sky until it was out of sight, the sliver of a moon revealing little through the sparse cloud cover rolling across the heavens.

As Santa stared up at the last place he could see the ascending robot from the Christmas star series of North Pole, Incorporated drones, he felt a disturbing presence nearby. Turning to his left suddenly, he barely avoided a swinging scythe blade, that was aimed at his neck. A large man, looking old enough to have served in World War II but still alive enough to be sixty was wielding the old, bladed farm implement, his grizzly beard in desperate need of a trim, or barring that, a wash.

"Get off my fuckin' land, asshole!" he shouted at Santa. "You fucking actors get carried away with yer Youtubing and Instagrams."

Taken aback, Santa just looked at the senile, violent old guy and shook his head. "What happened to you, Stan? You believed until you were thirteen!"

"And it ruined my life, tubby!" the ancient farmer shouted, swinging the scythe again, a look of pure hatred literally glowing in his eyes. "In middle school when they found out I still believed! They called me 'Santa Baby' all the way through high school!"

Glowing… Santa thought. *That means he's a…*

Santa jumped back as the old guy belched flames at him following his bladed swing, the greenish hue sickly looking. There was only one thing he knew of that hated Santa and belched green flames.

"You cannot stop me, Crank. Christmas is eternal," Santa said to the Holiday-hating demon possessing some person who had lost all spirit for the season.

"Get off my land, you faker!" the Crank screamed, blowing more fire from his lips.

Santa dodged this and rushed him. He plowed into him, grabbing the scythe's long wooden handle and using it to push the deceptive old guy back. A rock Santa had previously noticed jutting up from the soft earth five inches snagged the Crank demon's heel, spilling him backward and knocking him to the ground.

Crying out, the old man choked on the combustive contents that allowed his incendiary spew to exist in the first place. His throat began to bubble and glow as the flesh began cooking from the inside. It burst, burning holiday hatred erupting from the ragged burn hole, smoldering around the edges. He made horrible noises, and Santa took pity on him, granting him mercy from being a hate-filled curmudgeon ruined by his classmates far too long ago.

An extremely winter-savvy boot slammed down onto the Crank's head, crunching through it like a pumpkin just before its ripening. Gore covered the ground as it gushed freely from the Crank's ruined neck, pooling up between the leftover cornstalk mounds and running into the lanes between to form dueling, bloody puddles, side-by-side.

Santa sighed, his dismay at having to dispatch another Crank again this year evident on his face. It was getting worse and worse every December. So many didn't believe in Christmas anymore. It was depressing to Jolly Ol' Saint Nick, and he was not sure what to do about it.

A flashing caught his attention, as well as the rest of his reindeer, who began stomping in response to the newest message broadcast from the red-nosed son of Donner… or Blitzen, they never did get that paternity test. Santa looked up, the fallen Christmas star drone was about to pop.

"I should probably get in, eh?" he asked his wordless companions. "Methinks we will want to get off the ground as soon as possible before we get snowed in. About an inch or two should be sufficient."

The nine flying caribou from the world capital of Holiday Spirit nodded in agreement like a human being would. Then they too glanced up into the night skies. Santa got into the sled containing the famous sack of toys for the world's children. Finally, it happened.

A brilliant white explosion above blossomed into a mammatus cloud of epic proportions, arcs of lighting flashing on the outer reaches of the phenomenon. It swelled rapidly, spreading across the sky in a flood of gaseous precipitation that blotted out the thin lunar phase from sight. Thickening up more, the formation promised activity of a meteorological nature. Then it happened.

Snow began to fall. Lots and lots of snow. Downy, massive flakes that dropped steadily and straight to the ground, the absence of more than a breeze strange given the roiling snow clouds above. It was exactly what CUMULUS25 was designed for.

"Thanks, 25," he said.

Minutes later, Lightbulb Face was leading them up into the snowy heights to deliver his precious cargo to the children of the world, back on schedule once again and one less Crank around to taint the spirit of the season.

Then he shouted his catch phrase to the world below.

"Ho! Ho! Ho! Me-rr-rrrr-yyy Christmas!"

END

ABOUT THE AUTHORS

Christofer Nigro has been a lifelong fan of fantastic fiction in all mediums, from cinema to TV to prose to comic books to board games to video games etc. This includes horror, sci-fi, super-heroes, anime, tokusatsu, and pulp adventure. The public first saw his writing online with the original websites for Warrenverse: The Amazing World of the Warren Comics Characters and The Godzilla Saga; he also reconstructed the MONSTAAH website with the permission and blessing of its creator, Chuck Loridans (all three are slated for a refurbishment). He debuted as a published author with Black Coat Press in Volume 8 of its annual *Tales of the Shadowmen* anthology with subsequent stories in Vol. 9-19 to date, with no intention of stopping.

He has also had short stories published by Sirens Call Publications, Pro Se Press, Pulp Empire, Grinning Skull Press, Horrified Press, Local Hero Press, with Matt Dennion's self-published *Attack of the Kaiju Vol. 1: Age of Monsters*, and the charity anthology *Courage on Infinite Earths: A Kaiju vs. Cancer Anthology* to aid St. Jude Children's Research Hospital to battle childhood cancer. His first two kaiju novels *Dargolla: A Kaiju Nightmare* and *Megadrak: Beast of the Apocalypse* were published by Severed Press, with new editions planned from Raven Tale Publishing. He established Wild Hunt Press in 2018 to continue publishing his work and those of other authors.

Dustin Dreyling is an avid fan of science fiction and horror, with a soft spot for all things kaiju. Originally hailing from White Bear

Lake, Minnesota, he also likes proofreading novels, playing video games both old and new, and taking care of his planted freshwater aquariums. His first published story was featured in Zach Cole's linear horror anthology *The Experiment* from Wild Hunt Press, and his work can also be found in Wild Hunt's kaiju anthology *Attack of the Kaiju Vol. 2: The Next Wave.* His first novel, batch one of a kaiju horror series *Primordial Soup,* was released in 2020 from Wild Hunt Press. *Batch Two* is coming in 2023!

Also from Wild Hunt Press

The tragic saga of the angst-ridden teen werewolf starts here… and continues! Book 2 and 3 now available, with Book 4 slated for an early 2023 release!

A KAIJU THRILLER BY DUSTIN DREYLING

Primordial Soup

THE FIRST BATCH

WITH ILLUSTRATIONS BY
ELDEN ARDIENTE

Dustin Dreyling's debut novel, the horrific kaiju thriller of a series, starts here, with the second batch rampaging your way in 2023!

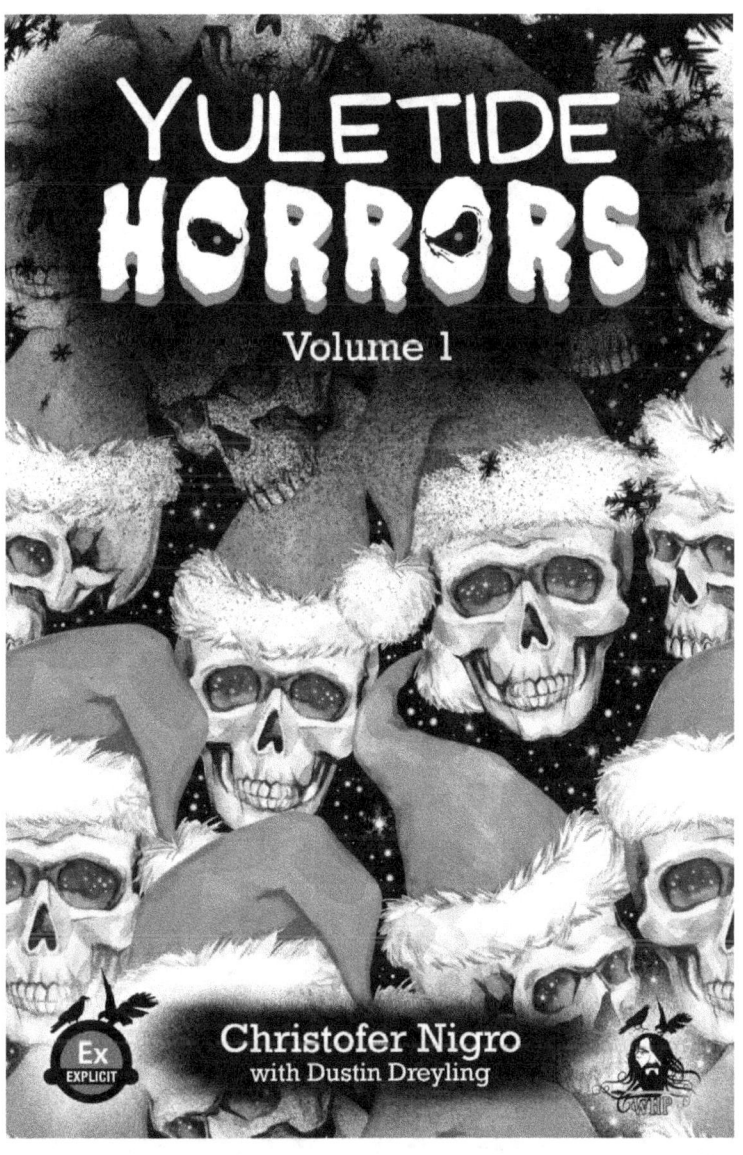

If one volume of seasonal horrors wasn't too much for you, and you're brave enough to come back for more, *Yuletide Horrors Volume 1* is still <u>on sale</u> at Amazon, and will be for as long as Christmas endures! And *that* is staying power!

www.ingramcontent.com/pod-product-compliance
Lightning Source LLC
Chambersburg PA
CBHW070533130626
46555CB00003B/1395